ONE MAN,
ONE MURDER

A KAYANKAYA MYSTERY

Praise for Jakob Arjouni

'It takes an outsider to be a great detective, and Kemal Kayankaya is just that'
– *Independent*

'A worthy grandson of Marlowe and Spade'
– *Stern*

'Jakob Arjouni writes the best urban thrillers since Raymond Chandler'
– *Tempo*

'There is hardly another German-speaking writer who is as sure of his milieu as Arjouni is. He draws incredibly vivid pictures of people and their fates in just a few words. He is a master of the sketch – and the caricature – who operates with the most economic of means'
– *Die Welt, Berlin*

'Kemal Kayankaya is the ultimate outsider among hard-boiled private eyes'
– *Marilyn Stasio, New York Times*

'Arjouni is a master of authentic background descriptions and an original story teller'
– *Frankfurter Allgemeine Sonntagszeitung*

'Arjouni tells real-life stories, and they virtually never have a happy ending. He tells them so well, with such flexible dialogue and cleverly maintained tension, that it is impossible to put his books down'
– *El País, Madrid*

Books by Jakob Arjouni

Happy Birthday, Turk! (A Kayankaya mystery)
More Beer (A Kayankaya mystery)
One Man, One Murder (A Kayankaya mystery)
Magic Hoffmann
Kismet (A Kayankaya mystery)
Chez Max
Brother Kemal (A Kayankaya mystery)

ONE MAN, ONE MURDER

A KAYANKAYA MYSTERY

JAKOB ARJOUNI
TRANSLATED BY ANSELM HOLLO

NO EXIT PRESS

This edition published in 2013 by No Exit Press,
an imprint of Oldcastle Books Ltd, PO Box 394,
Harpenden, Herts, AL5 1XJ, UK
noexit.co.uk
@NoExitPress

First published by Diogenes Verlag AG Zurich 1991
Translation from the German by Anselm Hollo 1997

ISBN
978-1-84243-831-2 (print)
978-1-84243-832-9 (epub)
978-1-84243-833-6 (kindle)
978-1-84243-834-3 (pdf)

2 4 6 8 10 9 7 5 3 1

Typeset in 12.25 on 14.5pt Bembo
by Avocet Typeset, Somerton, Somerset

Printed and bound by CPI Group (UK) Ltd, Croydon, CR0 4YY

For more information about Crime Fiction go to @CrimeTimeUK

ONE MAN, ONE MURDER

A KAYANKAYA MYSTERY

Chapter 1

I was at my desk, jotting down a dream line-up for the Gladbach football team on my calendar – and getting bored with Mr Kunze.

Borussia Mönchengladbach Dream Team:

Kleff

Hannes

Vogts   Frontzeck

Stielike

Bonhof   Simonsen

Netzer

Heynckes   Jensen   Laumen

Mr Kunze was my landlord. He was reciting to me, over the phone, all the reasons why my rent had to be raised next month by thirty per cent, and why life was not a bowl of cherries. 'Wife and children' was his groaning refrain. I placed Sieloff, Mill, Kamps, and myself on the reserve bench and seated Weisweiler, the coach, on a cloud. Then I interrupted Mr Kunze. 'Mr Kunze, if I understand you correctly, you feel that I'm the best tenant in the world, and if you had your druthers, you'd pay *me* a little something just to keep me on. On the other hand, your wife couldn't possibly make do with less than ten fur coats without coming down with migraines and making your life a living hell. That's all right. All of us have to look out for Number One. Nevertheless, I find a thousand marks for a one-room office with a sink – and regular power failures – a little excessive.'

'I agree! I quite agree! I always say that fifty percent of our quality of life consists of the quality of the workplace – the remaining fifty on our living quarters and personal relationships – those are, of course, the most important things. But just try to put yourself in my shoes: eleven buildings to take care of here in Frankfurt, a riding stable, four cars – you can imagine the taxes I have to pay! Then there's the repairs, and, and, and…'

I placed a cushion on top of the phone, retrieved a couple of Alka-Selzers from a desk drawer, tossed them into a glass of water and watched them effervesce, supporting my head with both hands. Under the cushion, Mr Kunze's voice sounded like a trapped bumblebee.

It was nine o'clock in the morning of the last day of March, nineteen hundred and eighty-nine. I had debts but no jobs. The tap was dripping, the coffee maker was busted, and I was tired. My office looked like a task force objective for Alcoholics Anonymous. Files and empty beer bottles lay scattered over floor and shelves. My deck of blank index cards smelled of spilled Scotch. The only wall decorations were a four-year-old Chivas Regal calendar and a postcard from the Bahamas. It was from a guy who cheated women out of their money with false promises of marriage. I had tried to track him down last autumn. On the card, he invited me to come celebrate his fiftieth birthday: '… my golden anniversary as a bachelor, as it were. It would be so nice to see you here.' The rest of the decor consisted of stained grey wall-to-wall carpeting dotted with cigarette burns, wallpaper yellowed by tobacco smoke, and the scattered remains of my exploded coffee maker. All things considered, a move might not be a bad idea.

I drank down my Alka-Selzers and went to the window. Full-fledged April weather: clouds charging across the sky like elephants. Once in a while a patch of blue, a sunny spell, then more rain. An old woman with a cane and a poodle was struggling along, keeping close to the wall. Children were swept down the pavement like empty plastic bags. A hat was sailing along in the gutter. The heat from the radiator caressed my knees, and I remembered my desperate and ruinous visits to offices of apartment buildings and landlords that one winter six years ago. By and large, these visits had followed a uniform pattern. It involved confronting a guy behind a desk who sat there, hands neatly folded, with a saccharine smile and ominously narrowed eyes, asking me in a manner that indicated he had better things to do: 'Well, then, Mr Kayankaya, I see you are a private investigator.

That's an interesting name… Kayankaya.'

'Not really that interesting. Just Turkish.'

'I see.' The saccharine content of his smile increases; his eye-slits are no wider than razor's edges. 'Turkish. A Turkish private investigator? What do you know… I hope you don't mind my asking, but – how come you speak such good German?'

'It's the only language I know. My parents died when I was a child, and I was raised by a German family.'

'But – but you are a Turk? I mean –'

'I have a German passport, if that makes you feel better.' His tongue darts out nervously to moisten his lips; then it disappears and modulates a voice that brings to mind innocent little kids skipping down a lane:

'Mind showing it to me?'

I hand him the little green book. He turns the pages. He subjects it to sub-molecular scrutiny.

'Not that we have any trouble renting to people of Turkish origin. And since you even are a German citizen… Nevertheless, we do have to know with whom we are dealing.'

He closes the little book and hands it back to me.

'I would have thought you came from one of the Arab countries. Your profile, your manner – you're not a typical Turk.'

'What is he like, your typical Turk?'

'Shorter, I'd say, more Asiatic, more inscrutable, somehow – well, just different.'

Is he going to rent me an office or isn't he? I clear my throat and ask. He is evasive, makes small talk, finally writes my telephone number on a scrap of paper that looks predestined for the waste paper basket. I take my leave. A week later, his secretary expresses his regrets.

I wiped cigarette butts and dead insects off the windowsill, leaned against it, my back to the window, crossed my arms and contemplated the office. 'A little clean-up, some new carpeting, and a new calendar,' I told myself. 'That could improve the quality of this workplace tremendously.'

When I lifted the cushion off the phone, Mr Kunze had hung up. A moment later, the doorbell rang. I hit the buzzer. The door opened, and in rolled a colourful sphere. Tasselled loafers, brown; white trousers, red belt; blue and white striped shirt; green tie with little dots; blue coat, big belly, short legs. Exuding *joie de vivre* from top to toe, he came to a halt just inside the door and scanned the office, looking perplexed. He just stood there and stared; and the longer he stood there, the less he seemed to know why he had come. Finally I said: 'What can I do for you?'

Cautiously, as if worried his shoes might get mouldy, he crossed the room, stopped in front of my desk, and ran his fingers through his hair. Then he adjusted his pink-framed eyeglasses and whimpered: 'My name is Weidenbusch. I would like to hire you.'

He really *whimpered*. Either his stomach exerted pressure on his vocal cords from below, or his collar was too tight; in any case, he whimpered like a puppy. My overall impression of him was that of your average schmuck from Frankfurt's West End. A guy who sips his red wine like a connoisseur even though he can't tell beer from Sprite, likes his underwear ironed, and thinks that pink eyeglass frames and colourful wristwatches are signs of an individualistic sense of style. All he would have needed to complete the picture was a carefully cultivated four-day stubble.

'To do what?'

'Well…' He cleared his throat, glanced around again. 'I hope I'm not bothering you in the middle of a move?'

A two-ton hint, that.

'No-a,' I growled. I picked up an empty cigarette pack, crumpled it and tossed it across the room. 'This is just my style.'

'Oh.'

He tried to respond to my smile. He almost managed that, and after we had smiled at each other for a while, and it began to seem as if we wouldn't be able to stop, I asked him: 'But surely you didn't come here just to discuss my office decor?'

'No, of course not…'

I pointed to the clients' chair. People who liked me called it an antique.

'Have a seat.'

He turned, took two steps, saw the chair, and stopped.

'But if you'd rather talk standing up…'

He nodded gratefully: 'You know, often it is easier to talk in a standing position.'

'Good, then. So, let's have it. I have a manicure appointment in half an hour.'

He took that without batting an eyelid.

'I'm sorry. You see, this is…' His eyes expanded to the size of plums. 'It's a case of kidnapping.'

'Of whom, or what?'

'My girlfriend.'

'When?'

'Today.'

I looked at my watch.

'Today?'

He nodded.

'I'm sure it has occurred to you that she might have a breakfast date, or an appointment with her hairdresser?'

'No, this is different – I mean, I know where she is.'

'I see. You know where she is.' I leaned back. Somehow, we seemed to be having trouble getting started. 'That's pretty unusual in kidnapping cases.'

He shook his head.

'You don't understand. I knew what she was planning, and… you see, she is…'

Once again, he adjusted his glasses. He did it all the time, or whenever he wasn't fussing with his necktie or running his fingers through his hair.

'… my girlfriend is from Thailand.'

He looked down. I arranged the wrinkles on my forehead to simulate thought. To liven things up a little, I asked him:

'And you forgot to pay the last installment? Or was she just a sample?' The question startled the human spheroid into a surprisingly lively spasm.

'I beg your pardon?'

'Never mind. Tell me more.'

He hesitated for a moment. Then he started pacing, giving me looks intended to make me feel like I had said something about his mother. The corners of his mouth twitched.

'Yes, she came from Thailand. But not the way you think.'

'I really don't think at all,' I mumbled, more to myself than to him. He nodded his assent. I almost began to like him.

'We met in quite a normal fashion, at a disco. Or that's the way it was, at first. She said she was on her way to visit relatives. Our first days together were like a dream.'

He went on to rhapsodise about the international language of love. Thai or German, feelings speak more than a thousand words, and so on. Then he seemed to reach an impasse; he sighed and fell silent. I stuck a cigarette between my lips and joined him. When it seemed to me that I had waited long enough, I asked: 'And?'

He looked up with an expression compounded of worry and longing. He raised his arms in a pleading gesture.

'Don't you see that I'm trying to tell you how important she is to me? You think I'm just one of those guys with a taste for Thai girls, but I'm not like that at all. I… You know, we just sat down together, just like that. She asked me a question with her eyes, and I answered by touching her…'

I slapped the desk with my palm.

'And just as you wanted to explain to her where the ladies' room was, she jumped out the window! For God's sakes, man, wake up! I can see that you're in love. Otherwise you wouldn't be here, suffering the pains of the damned because my office isn't furnished with little bistro tables… And I don't give a damn if she's from Thailand. That's your problem. But she has been kidnapped, and maybe I can help you find her again. Maybe – if you'll tell me what happened, instead of giving me all this bullshit about love's Esperanto.'

He opened and closed his mouth. His chin began to tremble. Then he closed his eyes, rubbed his eyelids with thumb and index finger, dislodging the pink glasses, and turned away from me. His shoulders shook. I sighed. At that moment, a burst of sunshine came through the window, and I felt like walking out into the street, into town, to have a beer. Instead, I scrambled out of my chair, went over to the multi-coloured sphere, and grabbed a shoulder.

'Stop driving yourself nuts. We'll find her.' His plum eyes looked up with a moist sheen. I grinned. 'And you'll regret that, soon enough. Both of you. At least when you've learned to speak the same language. Then there'll be no more touchy-feely jive – then you'll be discussing the soup, the shampoo, the weather report. No more palpitations and candlelight. Take out the garbage, and no more *World of Sport* for you.'

I couldn't tell if he was laughing but sensed a hint of that. I slapped him on the back and went back to my chair behind the desk. He sniffled a little more, and then, slowly, masticating his words as if they were a day-old bun, he continued his tale of woe. 'A week later I found out that she worked in one of those clubs. You know what I mean. I was very upset at first, but then I decided to do everything in my power to get her out of there. I visited her three times – at her workplace. It was terrible, truly terrible.' He shook himself. 'You can't imagine what that's like.'

17

'Right. Well…'

I wagged my head noncommittally. A saviour of whores, I thought. A candy-coloured, pink-bespectacled saviour of whores. And I'm supposed to help him because he's afraid he might catch something in one of those dumps. But I thought wrong, and this, in a concise form, was what he told me in the course of the next half-hour while padding back and forth in my office: He, Weidenbusch, had paid five thousand marks for Sri Dao, his girlfriend, a sum she allegedly owed the club for air fare, accommodations, and meals. Then she had moved in with him. After their days of wine and roses they began to consider the next move. Sri Dao's visa was due to expire in three weeks, and she had neither the means nor the desire to return to Thailand. An asylum appeal might prolong things a little, but it was one hundred per cent certain that it would be rejected. According to Weidenbusch, neither one of them wanted to get married. Unable to arrive at a decision, they let time pass, and her visa had already expired some days previously when they ran into a passport check. The police officer took Sri Dao's personal data and threatened her with deportation if she did not leave the country within the next three days. If Weidenbusch hadn't been with her, she would have been arrested on the spot. The following morning, as Sri Dao was packing her bags, the phone rang. A man who introduced himself as Larsson offered them forged papers for a price of three thousand marks. He told them they had half an hour to make up their minds. He would call back. Weidenbusch and Sri Dao decided to go for it and made the following arrangements with the caller: at seven o'clock next morning, Sri Dao would be waiting, with the money and a passport photograph, at a taxicab stand by the east entrance of the main railway station. Alone. A grey VW van would pick her up and take her to a secret destination where the papers were manufactured. Twenty-four hours later she would be returned to the Weidenbusch residence.

The pair did as they were told, except for one thing: Sri Dao did not arrive alone. The grey VW van drove up, a guy sporting a moustache and sunglasses jumped out, opened the sliding side door and shouted *'schnell, schnell'* to Sri Dao. At that moment, Weidenbusch stepped between her and the guy and demanded to be told where she would be taken. The moustachioed fellow shoved him aside and pushed Sri Dao, who was shouting 'No, no' and 'This is my man' in English, into the van, slammed the door shut and got into the driver's seat. Weidenbusch almost tore the passenger door off its hinges but had a pistol stuck in his face before he could utter a sound. It took only seconds for the van to disappear, and Weidenbusch found himself sitting on the pavement in a state of shock. At some point during the next hour it occurred to him to consult a private investigator, and here he was. Trembling and waving his arms he stood in front of me and said, over and over again: 'With a gun, a real gun – here,' and he pointed at the right side of his face, 'one false move, and…' He covered his face with his hands and shook his head.

I offered him a cigarette. He took it without even looking at it. Then he came to a sudden halt, stared at the thin white cylinder in astonishment, dropped it on the floor and stepped on it with his tasselled loafer. While I was still marvelling at his unexpected adaptation to my house style, he sank into my visitor's chair, stretched his legs, and gave a high falsetto command: 'I want to find her again, and I want you to rearrange that hoodlum's face!'

The bit about rearranging a face sounded as if he had memorised it for the day.

I concentrated on cleaning my fingernails with a match. 'How did you find me?'

He looked startled. His eyelashes fluttered irritably. He didn't say anything.

'You must have checked the Yellow Pages. But why Kayankaya, why not Müller?'

'Because she's Thai, and I thought...'

'You thought Thailand and Turkey both start with a T?'

'How could I have known that you're a Turk? On the contrary, I expected – but...'

Unfinished, the sentence hung between us as if someone had strung barbed wire across the room.

They visit exhibitions in New York and go on safaris in Africa; they smoke hashish in Cairo, eat Japanese food, and propose to teach democracy to the Muscovites; they are 'international' down to their Parisian underwear – but they're not able to recognise a Turk unless he's carrying a garbage can under his arm and leading a string of ten unwashed brats. I thanked my lucky stars that Weidenbusch was not my prospective landlord. I tossed the match on the floor and examined my fingernails. 'What's the name of the club your friend worked for?'

'It's the Lady Bump. On Elbestrasse.'

'And to whom did you pay the five thousand marks?'

'To a man called Korble or Koble…'

'Köberle? Charlie Köberle?'

'That's it.'

'Who else knew the expiration date of her visa?'

'Oh – a couple of friends, and my sister.'

'What does your sister do?'

'She works at a day care centre. She does therapy there, child therapy.'

'She's a kindergarten teacher?'

'Something like that.'

I fished out a cigarette and rolled it between my fingertips.

'You don't really look like a guy who'd fall for mysterious phone calls. You should have known that people like that aren't harmless pranksters.'

'But I wouldn't have agreed to it, if.' He gulped, closed his eyes for a moment. His hands locked together like a couple of fighting octopi. 'You see, yesterday morning, what with her bags all packed, everything happened so quickly, and then…' His shoulders sagged with exhaustion.

'Do you know anyone else who received an offer like that? Maybe one of her former colleagues at Lady Bump, for instance?'

'No, I don't.'

'All right. Two hundred marks a day, plus expenses. Your address, your phone number, where you can be reached during the day, and your girlfriend's complete name. I'll see what I can do.'

Five hundred-mark bills emerged from his alligator skin wallet and wandered across my desk.

'One more thing. I'm not into strong-arm stuff. If you need someone to rearrange faces – '

'No, no – I was just so excited when I said that. I'm sorry.'

I accepted his apology and took the money. 'Your profession?'

'Artist.'

I was dumbfounded. 'Huh?'

With an eager but nervous glitter in his eyes he explained: 'Yes, I'm a sculptor and painter. I write, too – short stories for television. I may even get to make a movie sometime soon. And I write things for the radio, as well.'

I stared at him. 'You do all those things at once?'

'I can't help it. I have to do things, I have to work and be creative. If I don't, I go nuts.'

'I see. You ever try television and beer?'

He gave me a sweet and sincere look and said in a confidential tone: 'I can't stand that. I really can't. I envy you for being able to do that.'

I wasn't sure he'd got my point, but I didn't really care. 'Your address?'

He handed me his card. A little flower on the left, a little flower on the right, and in the middle: Manuel Weidenbusch.

'Sri Dao Rakdee. Rakdee with two "e"s.'

I flicked the card with my thumbnail and said: 'See you later.'

Chapter 2

Frankfurt was covered by a blanket of rumbling darkness. The first raindrops started falling. I managed to more or less squeeze my Opel between two convertibles from Offenbach and ran up the steps to the Eros-Centre Elbestrasse. Two grey plastic flaps marked the entrance. They looked as if every visitor had stopped to puke on them before leaving the establishment. I pushed them aside and entered the ground floor. Tiled walls and floor, pink lighting. The walls decorated with bosomy plaster busts and joke paintings of the genre 'Hunter Pursues Stag While Stag Mounts Hunter's Wife.' Invisible speakers played 'Amore, amore' sung by a swoony Italian voice. The air was dense and sweet and seemed to move in waves as one walked through it. It was a depraved, gigantic *pissoir de luxe* in which the female attendants wore garter belts and colourful panties. Not far from the entrance, rows of doors stretched down half-dark hallways. Every few feet another door, and behind each door a room that smelled of sweat: a towel on the bed, porno pictures on the walls, a sink, a pack of Kleenex. Most of the doors were closed. In front of those that were open women sat on stools, bored and heavily made up, their legs stretched out into the hallway, their smiles as fake as glass pearls. This time of day, no one worked unless they had to. There were no clients except for a couple of weirdos who toured the hallways three or four times pretending that they had just wandered in by accident.

Tucked away in a corner was the establishment's own refreshment stand. Soft drinks and small sandwiches for the personnel. On the counter three flies were fraternising with the sandwiches under a glass bell. A small man wrapped in a blanket huddled next to the cash register contemplating a jigsaw puzzle, the unlit butt of a hand-rolled cigarette in a corner of his mouth. The puzzle seemed to represent the German Chancellor in fifty pieces. Next to the man stood a full glass of vermouth; at his feet lay a sleeping dachshund sporting a knitted vest. The shelf behind them held a row of dusty cans of lemonade.

'Slibulsky here?'

He shook his head without looking up. I watched him compose Herr Kohl's chin.

'Having fun?'

He shook his head again. Droplets of sweat were trickling down my neck. My palms were damp, the collar of my coat felt scratchy in the stifling heat. I was being boiled alive, slowly, and I found it astonishing that he had wrapped himself in that blanket.

'It's an easy one, just fifty pieces.'

He set the piece he was holding aside and turned to me. 'It's a freebie. From the party. I don't care for politics, but it's a freebie. *Capish*?' He sneered. 'Normally I do the ones with three thousand pieces. At least.' The cigarette butt stayed stuck to his lip and wagged up and down as he spoke.

He looked at me a while longer as if to say 'and if you'd like to be punched in the mouth, I'll be glad to oblige.' Then he turned his attention back to the puzzle. I smoked, he did his jigsaw puzzle. I checked the time. Quarter past eleven. I had agreed to meet Slibulsky at eleven sharp.

I had known Ernst Slibulsky for two years. We were almost friends. He fixed my car, I advised him on the choice of presents for his girlfriend, and whenever he'd had a fight with her, he came and crashed on my couch. Once a week we played billiards, had a couple of beers, talked about football. Sometimes we had too many beers, tried to discuss other subjects, and didn't agree about anything. Three months ago, Slibulsky had started working for 'Ibiza' Charlie. He bounced the johns when they got out of hand, he collected the money from the ladies. It was the first time he'd done this kind of work.

The small man sighed. The puzzle was done. He reached for the glass of vermouth but did not remove the cigarette butt while he drank. When he put the glass down, it was empty. He frowned, wiped his mouth with the back of his hand.

'Maybe this is so easy because it's designed for Herr

Kohl? So he can have a little relaxation when he's all worn out from governing the land.'

I yawned. He squinted up at me. 'Guess you're not easily amused?'

'Not when I haven't had enough sleep.'

Without averting his eyes, he lit the cigarette butt and leaned back in his chair. 'You a john?'

I shook my head. The tip of his cigarette glowed. He looked up at the ceiling. 'In the old days, I wouldn't have asked you that. In the old days, this was a decent establishment with decent girls. We had a sign on the door that said "No Tourists." Funny, huh?'

'A scream.'

He nodded thoughtfully. 'But now? Nothing but kaffirs and perverts. But it's no wonder, what with all the new diseases they're inventing in America.'

I dropped my cigarette on the floor and stepped on it. '"No Tourists"… Those were the days. You're a kaffir, too, aren't you?'

'One who's ready to rub these little sandwiches all over your ugly mug if you don't watch your mouth.'

That seemed to amuse him. 'Better not do that. You see, I'm Charlie's big brother. A little retarded, but his brother.'

'You don't seem all that retarded to me.'

'I don't?' He pulled the blanket off his lap. His legs were two short stumps. 'What do you say now?'

'I'd say you're pedestrianly challenged.'

'You would, would you?'

His laugh sounded more like a cough. It was ugly and maliciously gleeful. He picked up a bottle of white Cinzano from behind his chair and poured himself a refill.

'Yeah, I used to be a big shot. But then, one day – shazam! Both legs sliced off – like sausages. After that, Charlie got me this gig. Making little sandwiches for whores. Nice, eh? In this dump.'

'That's family loyalty for you.'

A draft of air. Slibulsky came tearing round the corner.

Short dark curls, hamster cheeks, boozer's nose. He was wearing a turquoise jogging outfit with sequins and carried a box of plastic 'surprise' eggs for kids under his left arm. His right arm was in a plaster cast.

'Morning, guys.'

The box landed on the counter.

'On special today. One mark apiece. So the girls have something to laugh about. Charlie had a brainstorm yesterday. He thinks this bordello needs a "friendlier ambiance."'

The man in the chair growled contemptuously. Slibulsky smiled at him. 'What's the matter, Heinz? Having a bad day?'

The cigarette butt, dead again, landed on the floor. 'Got out of bed on the wrong leg.'

Slibulsky grimaced noncommittally, turned to me, punched my shoulder with his left: 'So, Kayankaya, you've gotten over your defeat last Sunday?'

I nodded at his cast. 'Doesn't look like your victory did you much good.'

'Yeah, well… I fell down a flight of stairs. Forgot to tell you that when you called.'

'Is it bad?'

'Hardly worth mentioning.'

'What about the tournament?' He shrugged.

'Maybe you can practise left-handed shots? We can carve a groove in your cast, for the cue.'

'Figure-pissing is about all I can do with my left.'

We grinned.

'That would be something, wouldn't it: the tournament begins, Bierich and Glatkow and all those hotshots take their ivory cues out of their cases, and you get up and say 'Look here, folks, billiards isn't everything' and piss a nice sunset on the rug.'

Slibulsky flashed a smile. Then he mimed a bow and said in a loud voice: 'Thank you, gentlemen. Five pilseners on the house, and I'll sign for them.'

From under the counter came a drawn-out creaking sound. Then the dachshund started barking.

'Now you assholes woke up the dog! Shut up, Howard! I'm telling you, shut up! Goddamn dog – Howard!' Barks and roars crescendoed to unbearable decibels.

Slibulsky signalled to me, shouted 'Later, Heinz' at the battle scene, and we left the refreshment stand.

The Eros-Centre Elbestrasse had four floors, and on each floor there were twenty to twenty-five rooms, one shower, and one toilet. The first and second floor were swept every day; firmly in German hands, they were the busiest. Going up, the hallways grew darker, the women less expensive and more colourful. On the third floor, Asiatics, on the fourth, Africans; the cleaning woman came once a week. A separate street entrance led to Lady Bump in the interior courtyard, a dingy little bar with corduroy armchairs and a strip-tease stage. It was designed to give an impression of class, but except for the privilege of drinking champagne with the ladies and seeing one of them dance naked under coloured lightbulbs every half hour, conditions, prices, and rooms were the same as in the Centre.

Above all this, in a refurbished penthouse, were the quarters of Ibiza Charlie, one of the Schmitz brothers' managers. In addition to the Eros-Centre and the Lady Bump, Charlie also supervised a small porno movie house next door. As long as the monthly accounts satisfied the Schmitz brothers, Charlie was free to manage the three enterprises as he pleased. He was able to hire his brother to work the refreshment concession, to hire Slibulsky for the scheiss-work and two assistant managers for the bar and the movie house, and to spend his days riding around in his convertible, getting drunk, and going to the races. But if, one day, the accounts shouldn't please the Schmitz brothers, Charlie would be out on his ass pronto, or laid up in hospital, or – in the worst case – neither of the above, and nevermore. The brothers knew their business. Their business consisted primarily of their ability to impress everybody else with how well they knew it. They owned three other brothels in the district around the railway station, a dozen bars, several game arcades, and two furrier's shops. They were two big fish in that pond, and their connections to City Hall enabled them to walk over dead bodies. Eberhard Schmitz was the honorary president of the SPCA, brother Georg the director of the Mardi Gras Society Sachsenhäuser Narren Helau.

As we walked upstairs I asked Slibulsky: '*What* does he call the dachshund?'

'Howard, after Howard Carpendale. He's the favourite

singer of Heinz's wife. Heinz hates the guy, so that's what
he calls the dog.'

'His wife calls him Howard, too?'

'No. She calls him Heinz.'

We sidled past two johns who stood leaning against a
railing. They were staring at a closed door.

'Which name does the dog recognise?'

'Neither one. He's deaf.'

'Doesn't seem like they love him a lot.'

'Oh, they love the dog, all right.'

On the third floor, two Thai women retreated quickly
into their rooms as soon as they saw Slibulsky. We walked
up the next flight of stairs in silence.

'They seemed to be scared of you.'

Slibulsky stopped. His cheerfulness had evaporated.

'Don't we have an agreement?'

He was right. We had discussed the matter. Slibulsky
was able to earn some fast money here, as he himself put
it, and it was his intention to quit after a year to open his
own car repair shop. An old dream. I hadn't really cared;
the world would be none the worse for Slibulsky's
working in a brothel. On the contrary, its employees
probably benefited from his working there. Then again,
when we had discussed this I had not yet seen women
disappear behind closed doors when they caught sight of
him.

'You used to be a dealer. Strikes me that was a more
decent job.'

'More decent, eh? The last time they put me away for a
decent year in jail.'

I kicked a crumpled handkerchief down the stairs.

'What happened to that inheritance?'

Slibulsky looked at me reluctantly. 'Come again?'

'You told me about it last winter. Some grandma in Berlin was going to leave you a bunch of money.'

'Oh, yeah … That was a bust.'

'You don't say.'

'No inheritance. Nothing but debts.'

He looked out the window. Somewhere below us a door slammed.

Slibulsky turned toward the next flight of stairs and said: 'Let's go. Charlie's waiting.'

We didn't say anything during our final ascent.

A bar, a black leather couch and chairs, red light bulbs, a metal-frame table with a glass top, a bed covered in blue silk, framed heavy metal posters on the walls. A video/stereo/CD entertainment centre in one corner, a fluffy white rug on the floor. A thousand or so square feet of space with all the charm of a porno movie set. The window provided a view of the rooftops of the railway station district. To the left, the BFG building, to the right, the main station, a game arcade and a homeless shelter across the street. A ventilation unit hummed quietly. The air smelled of cleansing fluid. Ibiza Charlie sat on the couch in his red kimono, checked his Rolex, and yawned. His face was swollen and spotted. Red welts made his eyes look tiny. His neck was as thick as a sewer pipe. Charlie's head reminded me, to a regrettable degree, of a double helping of pork knuckles topped with a permed thatch of sauerkraut. He leaned back, eyes half closed, and ran his fingers through that hair as if it was time to impress the ladies. His kimono fell open, exposing a plump white belly.

I went to the window and lit a cigarette. Behind the bar, Slibulsky rummaged through cabinets and empty bottles on his quest for an eighty-proof liquid breakfast.

After Weidenbusch had left, I had made several calls and discovered that Sri Dao was not the only person who had disappeared. An Iranian and two Lebanese had been reported missing for two days from the asylum seekers' centre in Hausen. All three of them had deportation orders out on them. They could have gone underground even without forged papers; to tell the truth, I didn't really believe the forgery story. Then I had called Slibulsky and had asked him to arrange a meeting with Charlie.

With a sigh, Slibulsky came out from behind the bar, brushed dust off his trousers, and stated: 'The Asbach's all gone, and there's only a drop of Bacardi left. The beer is warm. So, Cola straight up, or eggnog?'

Charlie's lips curled in disgust. 'That slut!' He turned to me, man to man: 'Here I've been buying her goddamn underwear for weeks, taken her out to eat in the best beaneries, showed her a good time, spent money like I was seducing the Empress of China – and that fucking peasant cunt from Odenwald can't manage to keep a couple of beers in the icebox.'

He got up and stabbed the air wildly with his index finger. 'But that's all over now! Tomorrow she'll go to work. And that other one, the brown beauty, she gets fired tomorrow. I can't stand her whining anymore.' Waving his arms, he started striding around the room, his face set in a fixed stare. 'Is it my fault that her brats don't have anything to eat? Am I Jesus? What kind of mother is she, anyway, leaving her kids behind in the desert? I gave her a little lecture on Third World affairs, a while ago. I explained to her "no fucky-fucky, no baby, enough chappies in desert already" – it's as simple as that. So…' He stopped for a moment, mulled things over. 'Well, she smiles at me the way she always does and says 'No problem, Mister, no problem.' I say, 'Very big problem. You not make enough money, I kick you out in street.' And she just goes 'No problem, Mister.' So, what can I do? I'm responsible for making sure that this fucking business runs the way it's supposed to – and as long as I have any say in the matter, it will!'

He turned, grinned, and rumbled: 'Right, Ernst?'

Plaster cast, arm, and head propped up on the bar counter, Slibulsky looked bored. He nodded. For a moment, Charlie didn't react, but then his grin turned dangerous, and he slouched slowly toward Slibulsky.

'Listen, asshole, when I ask you something, I want to hear an answer. Understand? I want to hear it. Anything. "Yes, Charlie", or "Right, Charlie" – I don't give a shit. But I want some sound waves in my ear. And even if that requires a great big effort, I want you to open your goddamn mouth. Because I'm the boss here, *capish*?'

Slibulsky made a cotton candy face and said *'Capish,'* and, after a pause which could be interpreted a zillion ways, 'Boss.'

Charlie nodded, satisfied. 'That's it, little buddy.'

He patted Slibulsky's shoulder. 'No offence, now.'

He strutted back to the couch and sank back into it, his legs wide apart. He raised his eyebrows.

'People of character tend to be a little brusque in the morning; Sometimes in the evening, too. But especially in the morning.' He shrugged. 'Can't be helped.'

I cleared my throat. 'How about talking about my stuff for a change?'

He stared contemplatively at my shoes. Then he picked a small cigar from the table and flicked a golden lighter.

'Our little buddy has told me about it.'

The cigar crackled. Slowly, he turned his head toward me. 'Do I look like I need to cheat some poor girl out of her last pennies?'

'I don't know what you need. But it's not a question of pennies, it's about a woman who can make six or seven thousand marks a month in a brothel – not to mention the three thousand she had with her.'

Charlie took the cigar out of his mouth.

'I thought it was a matter of forged papers.'

'First of all, somebody knew when Sri Dao Rakdee's visa expired. And up to a couple of weeks ago, she was working here. For you.'

'Right.' He leaned forward. 'But I have enough girls here. I don't need to use dirty tricks. You have any idea how many of them show up daily, begging me to let them work here?'

'If you say so. And how many are being specially imported from Thailand? Before she could leave here, Mrs Rakdee had to pay you five thousand marks for her travel expenses.'

Thin-lipped now, he stared fiercely at me. 'And that's

because I have such a big heart. Let me tell you, Snoopy, before she came here she worked for a guy who didn't even give her enough to eat. And I lent her that money so she could buy her freedom.'

'What's his name?'

'What do you think I am? Some kind of information office?'

The hand holding the cigar sliced the air and slammed down on the glass tabletop. The cigar broke and bits of it scattered across the rug.

Charlie froze. 'Shit! My brand-new rug!'

He got down on hands and knees and frantically picked ashes and bits of tobacco out of the white fluff. I cast a 'check-this-out' glance at Slibulsky. Poker-faced, Slibulsky just stood behind the bar, drinking warm beer and looking as if he'd spent his entire life watching people picking tobacco crumbs out of fluffy rugs.

Still on all fours, half under the table, Charlie ranted: 'Jesus, Slibulsky, where do you find these guys, huh? I'm supposed to blow the whistle on people? What is this?'

Then he reared up, his face apoplectic. 'Or is it that you're a snoop, too? Some kind of dirty undercover cop? Planted here to find out if I do anything illegal? Come on, let's hear it!'

'But, Charlie...' Slibulsky tapped his forehead with his left index finger. 'No one would dare do such a thing to you. Everyone knows you can smell an undercover rat from a hundred yards.'

Charlie gave him a suspicious look. Then, satisfied, he growled and grinned.

'That's true. Someone would have to be very foolish.

35

Narcs don't stand a chance with me. I can spot them. Even if I couldn't see anything, or if it was dark all the time –'

'Blind, we call that.'

I waited until both of them had swayed in my direction.

Then I added: 'And now it's my turn to rant and rave.'

It really got quiet. Only a few street noises mingled with the hum of the ventilation. The thunderstorm had passed, and rays of sunlight danced through the room.

'You hit the nail on the head. I am a goddamn snooper, and I had hoped that you could tell me who, except for yourself, knows about Sri Dao Rakdee's visa. Slibulsky told you why I wanted to see you, and you agreed to see me, and I don't suppose you did that just so you could indulge in histrionics. So please pull yourself together and try to remember your reasons. We don't have to rush things, but with a little effort we may be done by lunchtime.'

Charlie stared at me as if I were a creature from another planet. Slowly he straightened his kimono and tightened the sash. Then he strode calmly toward me. Too calmly. Just as Slibulsky stuttered, 'Hey, Charlie, he didn't really –' his hairy paw landed on my shoulder. We scrutinised each other. Two tough guys in a tough world. One unable to make the rent, the other upset about dirt on his rug. There was a hint of a smile in the corners of Charlie's mouth, and the paw slapped my neck.

'I like you, snoop. Whenever you run out of suckers who need a detective because they can't do anything for themselves, you can always start working for me.'

I took the paw and handed it back to him. For a

moment, he didn't know what to do with it.

'I don't think that would work. I've got sensitive ears, and I'm not flat enough to use as a doormat.'

'Mouth as big as a barn door, eh?' He turned.

'Slibulsky – three eggnogs, and then you guys get outta here.'

I took a deep breath and tried to remember what eggnog tasted like and whether it agreed with my stomach.

We walked down the stifling staircase. A nubile voice was singing something about 'bodies in action'. The eggnog stuck to my ribs like glue. It also gave me the burps. The perfect drink for getting rid of people. It was invented by a host who wanted to let his undesirable guests know what he thought of them; he was probably the same guy who had come up with applejack, cherry liqueur, and Amselfelder Spätlese.

Slibulsky was leaping rather than walking, taking two steps at a time and well ahead of me.

'I told you it wouldn't be much use.'

'You tell Charlie that if I don't get the name of Sri Dao Rakdee's pimp, I'll call the cops on him.'

In mid-stumble, Slibulsky grabbed the bannister and swung back to face me: 'What did you say?'

'I'll tell them to shut the place down. Illegal personnel, drugs, dead bodies – I'll think of something.'

'Have you lost your marbles? I'll be out of a job.'

'If you don't want that to happen, you better come up with another idea. Ask around in the quarter. You know people who know these things.'

'Wait a minute! I never agreed to impersonate Dr Watson.'

'And I never agreed to come here to watch some half-crazed guy get out of bed.'

'You wanted to talk to Charlie, and you got to talk to him.'

Sparks flew between our eyes. I folded my arms across my chest and leaned against the flaking and faded black panelling that adorned the stairs and hallways. We could hear Howard Carpendale barking on the ground floor.

'And I wanted to call the cops if I didn't get that name by tonight. I still want to do it.'

'That's not fair.'

'A lot of things aren't. For instance, I knew from the start that Charlie wouldn't tell me anything. Why should he? He's a red-light district boss. I'm just a lowly private eye. Nothing in it for him.'

'Then why did he agree to meet you?'

'That's just it.'

Slibulsky frowned. He shook his head, looked down at the floor. 'You had too much to drink last night.'

Before I was able to respond, a Mr Supercharged approached us. A mountain draped in blue jeans, leather jacket, and black cowboy boots of a size my feet would disappear in. He was more than six feet tall, and his face consisted of nothing but hair: his beard, nose and head hair was a continuous dark brown rug. In the middle of the rug sat a pair of round mirror shades decorated with naked girlie stickers. His voice made the stairwell vibrate.

'Hey, man, Slibulsky, at long last! Everything's hunky dory, all I have to −'

Slibulsky coughed, loudly and drily. After he stopped coughing, he pointed at me and said: 'This is Kemal Kayankaya. He's a private investigator.'

Mr Supercharged raised his shades and checked me out without the slightest hint of embarrassment. Then he offered me his hand. It had a ring on every finger, including the thumb. Taken singly, those rings were just tasteless jewellery, but as a combo they served as a knuckle duster.

'Name's Axel. Ernst has told me about you…'

We shook hands. It was a bit like grabbing hold of a bazooka.

Slibulsky wiggled his feet. 'I'm just taking him down to his car. See you upstairs.'

Axel pushed the shades back into his rug-face, took his leave with a resounding 'All right,' and pursued his clanking ascent.

'Playmate of Charlie's?' I asked Slibulsky when we reached the pavement.

'Uh-hunh. He's all right, though. That's just his style.'

'Does he always stop talking when you cough?'

Slibulsky pretended to be watching an exciting pair of legs. They were exciting only if one favoured the kind encased in tight jeans and ending in basketball shoes, moseying along to indicate years of hiking experience.

'I asked you a question.'

'There are things it's better not to know.'

I opened my mouth but did not say anything. Then I tapped my forehead and walked to the Opel. Slibulsky reappeared next to me as I was unlocking the door.

'Is it my fault that you are a kind of cop? What happens

if someone wants you to snoop on me?'

I opened the door, stepped inside of it, and shrugged. A wave of stale air escaped from the car and enveloped us.

'OK, OK. Why not. Axel deals in stolen motorbikes. Sometimes I help him with the paint jobs.'

He looked at me. His jogging suit glittered in the sun. I got behind the wheel, closed the door, and wound down the window.

'I am not a cop. Don't worry about that pimp's name. Forget it, I'll find him some other way.'

I turned the key in the ignition. Slibulsky was chewing his lip. Then he turned and walked away, lost in thought. In the rear-view mirror I saw him collide with a parking meter.

Chapter 3

TURKISH PIGS A PLAGUE – I'M PROUD TO BE A GERMAN! I opened the door of the phone booth whose glass panes were covered, inside and out, with more of the same sort of drawings and statements, making it look like a favourite hangout of the juvenile delinquent SS. I lit a cigarette, took Weidenbusch's card out of my pocket and jammed the receiver under my chin. While I dialled, I read a spidery legend: 'Alf is German.'

Before the phone had rung even once, there came a breathless whine: 'Sweetheart?'

'No. Kayankaya.'

I could hear him gulp. 'Have you found her?'

'I may have a lead. Tell me, for whom did Mrs Rakdee work before she was employed at the Lady Bump?'

'You mean in Thailand?'

'No, here in Frankfurt.'

I told him about my visit to Charlie, and he seemed genuinely surprised. Sri Dao had indicated to him that she had arrived at the Lady Bump directly from Bangkok, via Frankfurt Airport. He said he didn't know anything about a pimp.

'Was it her idea to come to Germany, or was she hired by an organisation?'

'She didn't want to talk about that. She said those were just bad memories.'

'So all you know is that she came here at the end of December?'

'Why December? June.'

'June…?' I counted on my fingers. 'That's nine months. A normal visa is good for three.'

There was a moment's silence. He was probably torturing his necktie. 'You have to ask Köberle about that. He took Sri Dao's passport after she arrived and only handed it back to her in my presence.'

'Was the visa for the whole period, or had it been renewed every three months?'

'Renewed twice.'

'And when you pondered how to keep your friend in this country, it never occurred to you to figure out how they managed to renew the visa?'

He hesitated again. 'Yes, it did occur to me. I even wanted to go to the club and ask Köberle, but Sri Dao didn't want me to.'

'Why didn't she?'

'Because she was afraid of those people.'

'I see.' I dropped my cigarette on the floor and stepped on it. Through a curved letter L in 'Heil Hitler' I noticed a policeman who was circumambulating my Opel with evident interest.

I had double-parked it and left the engine running.

'Then I'd say there are two possibilities: either the visa stamps were forged, or your friend told the immigration service that she was getting married to a German citizen.'

'But I told you, Köberle kept her passport all that time.'

'Yes, that's what you told me.'

Hands clasped behind his back, the policeman now leaned into the open window on the driver's side.

'Just like you told me this morning that a marriage to her was out of the question. Tell me – why?'

While Weidenbusch was busy composing an answer, the policeman's green hat reappeared, and the head under it scanned all directions in search of the culprit. Setting his hands in motion, he pulled pad and pencil out of his shoulder bag and proceeded to write a friendly note from your fairy godmother.

'… I would have liked to marry her, but when I suggested it to her, she just shook her head. Later, she even got angry with me. It must be something to do with her culture.'

Right. Tribes outside of Central Europe didn't need reasons for their actions. They had 'cultures.' Now the cop was scrubbing dirt off my registration sticker.

'All right. I'll be in touch when I have news for you.'

'Will you get her back?'

'I will. Don't worry. Talk to you soon.'

Before he could say anything else I hung up and ran across the street.

'OK, OK! I'm back! You can toss that ticket!'

He looked up, surprised. He had just started lifting a windscreen wiper to place the ticket under it.

'I'm leaving. Just had to make a quick phone call.'

'So? It's illegal to park in a traffic lane.' He snapped the windscreen wiper down over the ticket, straightened his back and adjusted his hat. 'And let me tell you something, young man. You need to improve your attitude.'

'I don't need any advice on attitude from my employees.' While he glared at me, uncomprehending, I opened the car door.

'Just think about it for a moment: I'm paying you a salary for writing tickets so the fines can be used to pay others who write me more tickets, and so on. In that sense, and as far as I'm concerned, traffic cops are a total loss. Nevertheless, I keep on paying my taxes every year so that you can have an apartment, buy schoolbooks for your kids, and go to the movies. Now, think about it – would you go on paying someone who keeps kicking you in the ass?'

He looked at me as if I had lost all my marbles, or as if I had never had and was never likely to have any. I pointed my finger at him across the doorframe. 'See what I'm saying? But I keep on paying. How about a conciliatory gesture? How about tearing up that ticket?'

No reaction. Unchanged, frowning, one eye slightly narrowed, he stood there as if he hadn't heard or understood my question.

'Oh, forget it!' I got into the car and leaned out the window. 'Loitering in the sun, wearing those threads paid for by the state, and bothering people – some would call that "workshy" behaviour.'

Ten minutes later I parked across the street from the immigration office, slammed the door, and ripped the ticket from under the windscreen wiper.

The offices for names beginning with the letters K to R were on the third floor, in the left-hand hallway, behind the cocoa machine. The hallway was full of people of all pigments, standing, sitting, or lying down, all waiting for their number to come up. There were no benches or chairs. The floor was littered with cigarette butts and botched application forms. Faded posters advertised St. Paul's and Town Hall – FRANKFURT AM MAIN, CITY OF SIGHTS TO SEE – and above the doors, digital counters showed the current numbers. A video game noise emitted by invisible speakers replaced the old 'Next, please'. People weren't talking much, and only in hushed tones, perhaps because they felt that it was necessary to ration what air remained in the fog of sweat and stale smoke. Due to security regulations, windows could not be opened.

I sat down on the floor and leaned against the wall, between an adolescent disco gigolo to my left who kept himself frantically busy smoking Marlboros and fixing his hairdo and a Polish couple and their son to my right. Dad and Mum were nodding out over the daily paper, the kid whiled away the hours making two plastic cowboys go 'bang,' 'zong,' and 'pow'… I felt like going 'pow' on him, myself.

Suddenly two men in uniform ploughed through and past all the legs, children, and bags, disappeared in the office for S, and soon thereafter dragged a young black man down the hall and down the stairs while he kept protesting in broken German that he hadn't known about the deportation order. The people waiting followed him with their eyes as if he were an apparition. There was a moment when it looked like everybody was about to say something, but then they just looked at each other and remained silent.

It occurred to me that the posters advertising Frankfurt were not only in poor taste, but – as far as this office was concerned – completely counter-productive. The interests of the immigration authorities would have been better served by pictures of beaches in Beirut – MARBLE, ROCK, AND BROKEN IRON – or desert landscapes in Ethiopia – THERE'S NOTHING LIKE HOME COOKING. A campaign to further national loyalty to crisis areas. One could even conceive a double-barrelled approach, with, let's say, a picture of a Thai girl flanked by her parents – WELCOME TO THE FAMILY – this would not only encourage locals to return home, but would also appeal to the German male on vacation… Although it was true that the latter rarely set foot in this building. The video arcade noise interrupted my train of thought, and my number appeared on the display. I entered a standard office with standard furniture, postcards on the walls, potted palm trees by the window. The fortyish woman behind the desk was eating a cake. She wore a platinum blonde wig, a pink blouse, and a gold chain with an Eiffel Tower pendant. Her face was long and narrow and slightly remorseful, and when she spoke, it sounded as if she were reciting an instruction manual for disposable cigarette lighters. The room smelled of one of those perfumes designed to appeal to several tastes at once.

When she was done chewing and had wiped her

mouth thoroughly, she picked up a pen and looked at her pad. 'Number one hundred and eighty three?'

'Right.'

She made a check mark. 'Name?'

'Kemal Kayankaya.'

'Spelling?'

'Pretty good, mostly. I have a little trouble with those foreign words.'

She looked up and pursed her lips in a stepmotherly fashion. After she had scanned me and come to a conclusion, she hissed: 'The spelling of your name!'

I spelled it for her. Without lifting her pen, she asked: 'Nationality?'

'FRG.'

'Germany,' she corrected me under her breath. Then she looked up again, quite irritably. 'German…?'

'You want me to spell that?'

Her left eyelid twitched. While we glared at each other, she pushed the pad to one side and leaned back in her chair, holding on to the armrests.

'If you are a German citizen, Mr –'

'Kayankaya. How long have you been doing this?'

She looked startled.

'I don't think that's any of your business.'

'I was just thinking… If every name that doesn't sound like Wurst takes you that long to memorise, you may not be cut out for this job.'

Her forehead began to turn pink.

'One more crack out of you, young man, and I'll call security. If you really are a German –'

'I'm a Turk with a German passport.'

Her eyes flashed briefly. She saw an opening. She said: 'You mean you're a permanent resident? Seems to me you're a little confused.'

I began to get hot under the collar.

'If I had meant to tell you that I'm a permanent resident, I would have told you so. But that's not what I told you. I told you something else – remember?'

Instead of replying she held on tighter to the armrests of her chair and looked as if she was visualising my being drawn, beheaded, and quartered. In an adjacent room, a voice rose to a roar: '... you no understand nothing, I don't give a shit! Here you speak German, no nigger English!' Then someone banged on a table, then there were footsteps, a door opened, another voice giggled, and this was followed by murmurs and finally silence. The woman in front of me was still hanging on to her chair, her face contorted by fury, and seemed oblivious to all the commotion.

I pointed at the wall: 'Lovely manners.'

'We're only doing our job.'

'Why is it always "only"? Have you ever given that any _'

She let go of the armrests, leaned forward, and hit the desk with both fists: 'Get out of here!'

I shook my head.

'We're not done. I came here to enquire about my fiancée, Sri Dao Rakdee. Rakdee with two "e"s. She is from Thailand. We were going to get married last week, but we still haven't received the necessary papers. I wanted to know if it would be possible to extend her visa by another month?'

She seemed surprised by the question. Then she smiled triumphantly and told me, in a saccharine tone of voice: 'No, that's impossible.'

She reached for her cake fork.

'All right, then. Would you be so kind as to get Sri Dao Rakdee's file and note that,' I got up to look at the nameplate on her desk, 'Mrs Steiner has rejected an application for extension of her visa? So that I can inform my attorney.'

She put the fork down, chewed and thought this over for a moment. Then she pushed her chair back from the desk and got up. 'It'll be a pleasure.'

She left the room. I went over to the window feeling pretty good and lit a cigarette. I thought I had reached the end of the trail. Whether Sri Dao Rakdee's first German was a pimp, as Charlie claimed, or one of those guys who liked mail order brides, his name had to be in that file; and Mrs Steiner would hardly miss the opportunity to beat me over the head with it, to justify calling me a liar and a criminal and throwing me out of her office.

There was no other explanation for a visa extended twice for periods of three months. It all fit together. According to Weidenbusch, Sri Dao had shouted 'this is my man' during the fracas next to the VW van. Contrary to Weidenbusch's fond assumption, it had not been her intention to express her readiness to defend *him*. No, she had simply referred to her 'man', to the guy who had brought her to Germany and had promised marriage both to her and the authorities; who had then lost interest in her and sold her to the Lady Bump outfit. That guy knew when her visa expired and what brothel keepers were willing to pay for her. Today he had picked her up, with a three-thousand-mark bonus, in order to sell her again.

Given all that, there could be several possible reasons for Sri Dao's rejection of Weidenbusch's marriage proposal. First: her memories of the other guy were such that the mere word 'marriage' made her nauseous. Second: she was willing to risk deportation to keep her previous story a secret from Weidenbusch. Or third: she suspected that the immigration authorities would not approve such a change of bridegroom and therefore reject any further attempt to extend her visa.

So all I needed to do now was to look up the name of the guy in the phone book. Then I could return Sri Dao to Weidenbusch this evening, if not sooner.

Five minutes later, Mrs Steiner returned, flanked by one of her colleagues from security. She slammed the door shut and wagged her chin at me: 'That's him!'

The colleague was in his forties, balding, his few remaining strands of hair plastered sideways across the top of his skull. He wore a pale blue bomber jacket with a plethora of gold-coloured zippers. He gave me the once-over. Then he pushed his thumbs under his belt, hitched up his trousers, cleared his throat and stepped closer so that his fat face was a yard from mine. He flashed his teeth and spoke in a rapid-fire machine gun rattle: 'What's your name, nigger?'

So, I said to myself, this must be their guy with the communication skills. I took the cigarette out of my mouth and studied its glowing tip for a moment. His beery breath struck my face. I looked at him and said very quietly:

'Listen, pig. Another word out of you, and I'll see to it that you won't be able to stand up, sit down, or fuck – ever again.'

While Mrs Steiner suppressed a scream, my threat seemed to have the desired effect on her colleague. He was speechless. However, it didn't look like this situation would last very long, so I added: 'Where is the file?' Just as quickly came the reply from a safe distance: 'There is no file for Rakdee.' Mrs Steiner had one hand on the doorknob; the other hovered in the vicinity of a vase. I kept glancing back and forth between them, a proper little Hawkeye.

'If you're not telling me the truth…'

'I beg your pardon…!' Despite her obvious fear that our argument might turn into a free-for-all, Mrs Steiner looked indignant. 'I am a civil servant.'

In other circumstances I would have grinned, but now it seemed important to get closer to the door. The security guy looked like he'd explode any second, and I didn't feel like getting punched. On the other hand, I had better things to do than jail time for grievous bodily harm.

'All right, that's all I wanted to know. You could have saved yourself all this excitement. And if you want to know my name, there it is, on her pad. Take a good look at it. If we ever meet again, I would like to be addressed correctly.'

Now the guy looked like his head and shoulders were about to burst. He stood leaning forward a little, arms bent like a wrestler's, ready to pounce. Mrs Steiner stepped aside, I grabbed the doorknob and touched my forehead. 'Thank you all.'

I pulled the door shut behind me, stepped over the Polish kid who was still busy with his gunfighters, and ran down the stairs. Nothing happened until I had reached the landing below. Then a roar came from above, and I picked up speed. A guy in uniform met me at the exit.

'Hey, hey, what's the rush?'

'Be right back. I'm illegally parked…'

Before he was able to react, I was out the door and ran to the Opel. Seconds later, the security guy and the one in uniform charged out into the street. I slid way down in my seat and waited until they gave up and trotted back into the building. I started the car and drove off.

At the first refreshment stand I saw I bought a paper cup of coffee and a bar of chocolate and took them back to the car. So much for my theory, I thought; the stamps in Sri Dao Rakdee's passport were forgeries, provided by Charlie or someone else. She had been in this country illegally for at least six months. As far as her former guy was concerned, my only proof of his existence was a statement made by a half-crazed pimp. In her situation, forged papers or stamps had been her only recourse. Which left 'Mr Larsson' who had a moustache and drove a VW van. There could be a hundred reasons why he knew the dates of Sri Dao's visa. Maybe he wrote poetry in his spare time and belonged to Weidenbusch's circle of acquaintances.

I drank my coffee and decided to drive to the asylum seekers' centre in Hausen.

Chapter 4

A field the size of two football fields, covered with gravel, stretched out beside the road. At the far end, its boundary was marked by the buildings of a sawmill. Spaced out at regular intervals on the field stood metal containers, twelve feet wide, forty feet long, and a little less than ten feet tall – three rows of twenty. In the walkways between them tall streetlights rose out of the gravel. Each container had one door, one window, an outside toilet, and a washing line. On top of some containers lay piles of what looked like broken bicycle parts. On closer examination, these turned out to be homemade television antennas. Between the containers, children were playing games, men were sitting on folding chairs. The area was surrounded by a three-foot-high wire mesh fence, and the air was filled with the incessant screeching of sawmill machinery: auditory smog.

I walked along the fence to the entrance and its red and white barrier. Right next to it stood the administration building, a two-storey prefab with faux half-timbering and a flower bed of pansies complete with garden gnome – as if it wanted to show the refugees, when they came to get their daily mail, the cozy German idyll to be defended against their 'flood'. I walked along a newly laid path of 'natural' paving stones to the building and into the front office. The office was empty except for two goldfish in a bowl on the counter. Next to the counter was a bell-rope with the sign PLEASE RING, amplified by a drawing of a stick figure pulling a rope and causing musical notes to fly through the air to summon another, smiling, stick figure.

I pulled the rope and lit a cigarette, watching three adolescents amble toward the entrance. One of them was carrying a boom box.

'Can't you (she said *du*) read? There's no smoking here!' I turned around and almost fell through the window. Instead of the customary gatekeeper in shapeless uniform and television-induced daze, I confronted Miss Hospital. Her face was narrow and cleverly made up, she had huge brown eyes, and her blonde hair had been pinned up carelessly, as if she had just got ready to take a shower. Her luxuriant measurements were covered by a starched and ironed nylon uniform with a Red Cross emblem. On her, even clogs would have looked sexy.

I removed the cigarette from my mouth and took care not to stare at her breasts.

'Normally I'm a little sensitive about that, but if you insist…' I grinned, 'I don't mind your using the familiar form of address.'

For a moment, she looked surprised. Then she said coolly:

'I'm sorry, I mistook you for one of the residents.'

'Are you the director?'

'I'm the nurse on duty. Mr Schafer is not here.'

'My goodness. Compared to the nurses where I had my appendectomy —'

'No one has asked you to compare. Your cigarette —'

'Oh, yes.' I went to the door and flicked the butt into the pansy plantation. A mistake. I heard a sharp intake of breath. I wasn't doing too well in my endeavour to find out something from her. I took care to close the door without breaking the glass or the doorknob.

'Two days ago, three men disappeared from here. I would like to know if, before that, they received any unusual visitors or phone calls.'

'Are you a police officer?'

'Kemal Kayankaya, private investigator.'

She raised her eyebrows. 'Private investigator?'

'Oh, you know, one of those really tall guys with broad shoulders and a chin like a gun butt.'

Her expression remained impassive. Then she took another look at me, and I saw that I had managed to make her smile.

'Oh, yeah.'

I nodded. 'So, what can you tell me about those men?'

'You have to talk to Mr Schafer about that. I'm not allowed to give out that kind of information.'

'And when will Mr Schafer be back?'

'Next week.'

'Next week…?' It was Tuesday. I looked out the window. Two women with scarves round their heads were dragging a tub full of laundry across the square. 'Well, then

I'll just have to ask the folks here in the camp.'

'The *centre*. And besides, you won't be able to do that. Strangers are not allowed on the grounds. Unless you're visiting someone in particular.'

'Well, then I'll visit someone in particular.'

Unruffled, she stepped behind the counter and picked up a pad and a pen. A blonde strand of hair fell across her face. She pushed it back behind one ear with a gesture that seemed to threaten that strand with the scissors next time.

'Name and dwelling number?'

I looked at the goldfish. I was beginning to feel that I should have just enjoyed them and gone away.

'Listen, nurse, I'm sure you're doing everything by the book, but this happens to be a criminal case, and I can't wait a week or play games with you. So, if you don't want me to walk around your centre, then please let me have some answers. No one will know about it, and I'll forget that I ever saw you.'

A pause. She put the pen down and looked up. Then she raised her eyebrows. She said 'Oh, really?' And smiled, the second time.

A little later, certain that I was on the trail of a gang of forgers, I squeezed past the red and white barrier back onto the road. Last Friday, the three men had been notified of the rejection of their appeals for asylum, and of deportation orders effective immediately. On Saturday, Miss Hospital had received and transferred a call from a Mr Larsson, and on Sunday they had found the centre's safe ransacked and the trio gone. We had not managed to exchange phone numbers – or only unilaterally and rather unsuccessfully. She had tossed my card into a tray marked 'Orders for Electrical Appliances: Television Sets, Washers, etc.'

Clapping my hands over my ears against the screeching of the saws, I ran back to the Opel. Two silent children pressed their faces against the wire mesh and watched me get in and drive away.

Chapter 5

For the second time that afternoon, I entered the brown immigration service building. Ready for trouble, I approached the uniformed guy checking IDs at the entrance. Apparently there had been a change of guard; this was not the same fellow who had pursued me into the street. After giving me the usual suspicious up down up − left side right side − deep into eyes − well all right then look, he let me pass without further ado. I ascended past the floors crowded with applicants to the superintendent's offices. An empty corridor. My footsteps were loud. 'Department of Residence Violations − Superintendent Höttges, inspector Klaase' read the sign next to a door. I knocked.

'Come in.'

Two men surrounded by more of the typical fibreboard furniture. One of them in his mid-thirties: moustache and turtleneck, the other twenty years older: grey hair and necktie. They were sitting behind their desks, facing each other, and my first impression was that they had been sitting there since they were born, waiting for the other to finally stick his fingers into the outlet below the light switch. A pile of daily papers lay on the desk to the right, and the one to the left was graced by a framed photograph of a family at a shooting range.

The younger one nodded to me and said 'Hello.'

'Hello. Superintendent Höttges?'

He pointed to his opposite number who, after closing a file folder in a decisive manner, turned his face toward me. It was a bony, thin-lipped face with angular cheeks and a firm jaw.

For a moment he seemed to vacillate between just telling me to get out and listening to my nonsense first.

'What's up?'

'My name's Kayankaya. I'm a private investigator. I would like to enquire if you know anything about a gang of passport forgers who target rejected asylum applicants and illegal aliens to offer them their services.'

'They *target* them?' His cold grey eyes held mine. 'How do they do that?'

'Well, for instance, by finding out about current cases from various refugee organisations.'

'And what is your interest in this?'

'I am looking for a woman who accepted such an offer.'

'Her name?'

'Erika Mustermann.'

Out of the corner of my eye I watched Inspector Klaase.

He looked amused. Höttges remained poker-faced. 'Very funny.'

'No funnier than your question.'

'There is no gang like that.'

'You mean you have no idea?'

He closed his mouth firmly enough to indicate he wouldn't open it again until it was time to go home. He contemplated his hands, folded in front of him on the desk. His thumbs were tapping against each other.

'No, that's not what I meant.'

'All right, then. But perhaps you've noticed a recent increase in forged papers – or received information about some place or workshop where non-Germans congregate, regularly and for no obvious reason? The general public is pretty good at noticing such things.'

Höttges did not reply, and for a while the only sound was the tapping of a typewriter next door. Just as I had decided to call it a day, the young inspector cleared his throat and said, quite cautiously: 'There was that thing in Gellersheim –'

Höttges's stare struck him like a lightning bolt. Still looking at him, Höttges raised his hands, put one on the armrest of his chair and used the other to tweak an ear lobe. I was amazed by the menace with which he charged that simple gesture.

'Don't you have anything better to do, Klaase?'

'But boss, I –'

'Superintendent, if you please.'

The inspector's mouth fell open for a moment. Then he sighed, reached for a file, and sank deeper into his chair.

'As for you, Mr –'

'Kayankaya.'

'Your visit is over.'

I nodded. 'I get it.'

Inspector Klaase empathised with a quick glance across the top of his file. I winked at him, took two business cards out of my pocket and stuck one each on their desk lamps. 'Just in case you happen to be in a better mood one day and say to yourself, that nice young man who showed up this morning, we really should –'

'Out!'

Chapter 6

It was raining again, and as I drove up I saw how the rain was falling right into my apartment. It seemed that I had forgotten to close my windows when I left that morning. I parked the car and rushed across the street and through the front door. As usual, the greengrocer emerged from his apartment at that very moment. To avoid the usual bickering about my radio being too loud, my careless disposal of garbage, or my habit of showering after ten in the evening, I sped toward the staircase. But before I reached the safety of the first landing, he came charging round the corner behind me and for the first time in our shared history of pain and suffering shouted a friendly 'Good morning, Mr Kayankaya!' I almost fell on my face. I turned slowly and gave him a sceptical look.

'Not feeling quite yourself today?'

'Quite the contrary…' He came up the stairs with quick little steps, fussing with his hands. 'I just wanted to ask you for a little favour.'

I kept wondering if someone had put something in his coffee.

'Come on, friend. You're not supposed to know words like that.'

'But Mr Kayankaya…' A conciliatory smile. 'Let's just forget all that old stuff.'

'Let's not. And besides, my apartment is flooding.'

'Just one moment, please!'

He moved up one step so that we stood face to face and I could smell the gravy and apple sauce of his dinner.

'Let me tell you what this is about. Several tenants, myself included, would like to put up a billboard on the front of the building, but we need the landlord's permission. And so, to convince Mr Kunze of the worth of our endeavour, we've been collecting signatures for a petition – and yours would be particularly important.'

'A billboard?' I gaped at him. 'To advertise cigarettes or margarine or – ?'

'No, but one proclaiming… shared goals and values which we would like to make known to the public, or in this case, our street.'

'What kinds of values?'

'Political and social ones, but philosophical ones as well, concerning humanity as such.'

'Have you gone nuts? What is it you want up there on the wall?'

'Well, you see… I hope you won't be prejudiced… To cut a long story short, we are members of the district association of the Republikaner Party, and we would like to provide the party with some thought-provoking publicity.'

I breathed out slowly. Then I asked: 'Who's 'we'?'

'My wife and I. The theme of the first series of billboards will be: Germany – so great –' he beamed at me, 'that there's room even for our guests.'

'Who has signed your petition?'

'Until now, everyone I've asked. People like the theme. Mrs Augstein on the fourth floor, Mr Walser, and that young couple, Knapp and Kretschmann.'

The faces attached to those names appeared to my mind's eye.

'An alcoholic lady, a senile guy, and two idiots – quite a team. What about the Benmessous, or Mr Karagiannidis?' He retreated three or four steps. 'Or the Metins, who buy at least half of your miserable vegetables? Have you asked them, too?'

'Yes, but –' He put more steps between us; I followed, and slowly we progressed back down to the ground floor.

'– but it looks like they haven't managed to shut you up. Or maybe they felt sorry for a pitiful asshole like you.'

He stumbled around the end of the bannister and looked at me through the black iron railing. The corners of his eyes twitched.

'Here one tries to be open-minded –'

I came at him, and he turned and ran to his apartment door. Half hidden by the doorframe, he wagged his index finger at me and shouted: 'So now we're being threatened in our own building! But just you wait! When we get to run the show…' The door slammed. Silence.

I stood there for a while. It occurred to me that if this was an example of the courage and intelligence with which Republikaners pursued their goals, their party wasn't long for this world. On the other hand, I had always regarded even that old souse Mrs Augstein as slightly off the beam but nevertheless capable of making distinctions.

Since I was sure my bed would be soaked by now, I walked back to the mailbox and pulled out a bundle of bills and junk mail. I did not notice the handwritten note.

In my apartment I tossed the mail on the bed and closed the windows. Then I went to the kitchen, checked the freezer, and picked the beef goulash. I unwrapped the package and tossed the frozen brick into a saucepan. Just as the stovetop began to make sizzling noises, the phone rang. On the way to my chair I picked up a fresh pack of cigarettes and opened a beer. I made myself comfortable and picked up the phone. 'Kayankaya.'

'This is Klaase.'

'Oh, Inspector – I had been hoping you'd call.'

'I thought so, too. Found your number in the book. The old man took your business card.'

'He's quite the sergeant-major, isn't he?'

'Not too bad. He throws the occasional fit, but we get along most of the time.'

'Mhm.'

'But after you left, I remembered... You're the detective who caught Superintendent Futt, a few years ago?'

'Yes.'

'I was impressed, even though he was a colleague.' He chortled. 'Maybe because I was one of Futt's trainees.'

I laughed a little just to make him feel good. Then I asked: 'What about Gellersheim?'

'We got a complaint last night. One Olga Bartels claims

that for six months, at regular intervals, large groups of foreigners have been brought to stay in the villa next to hers. Always different ones, and they always stay only three or four days.'

'Whose villa is it?'

'No idea. We didn't do anything about it.'

'Why not?'

'Because we get complaints like that every day, and the old man said he was sure this woman was just another one of those alarmists who have nothing better to do than stay glued to their front window all day.'

'That's how he put it?'

'More or less.'

'The address?'

'Number six Am Rosenacker.'

I jotted it down on a television magazine and sipped my beer.

'If you get so many complaints, why are you telling me about this particular one?'

'Because it involves larger groups, and because of their short stays. Normally, the complaints involve families or single persons whom people suspect to be in hiding.'

'Is there anything you can tell me about forged papers?'

'Nothing special. The usual amateurish stuff: erased dates, altered photos, and so on.'

'Well, then, Inspector, I'm much obliged.'

'Don't mention it. We're all doing our job. And don't mind the old man. He hasn't had such an easy life.'

I hung up. Gee, I thought: was that the immigration police or the Salvation Army?

On the TV, McEnroe was wiping out a taciturn Swede.

I drank my beer and watched him tell a female umpire something about his backside. I wished that Sri Dao would reappear that evening: case closed. The villa in Gellersheim was probably inhabited by a wealthy family that really enjoyed vacations. Tanned faces and frequent absences must have given Mrs Olga the impression that this had to be a nest of gypsies.

Ten minutes later, the goulash was warm. With some bread and a plateful of the stew I sat down to the tie break. Six five. Six six. Double fault McEnroe, six seven. The Swede's turn to serve. I spilled goulash on my trousers. Second serve – return on the line, seven seven. The bread was turning back to dough between my fingertips. Long exchange, McEnroe to the net, save of the century – eight seven! Deep breath. Change of service. Left and right forearm raised to forehead. Take position. Not a sound. Serve, ball in court, backhand return, half-volley, lob, smash, the Swede leaps – and misses. I detached the bread from my fingers and picked up the spoon again. At the beginning of the second set, the doorbell rang.

'What do you know.'

'I happened to be in the neighbourhood and thought I'd look in…'

I held the door open. 'If it doesn't bother you to watch tennis with a cop.'

Slibulsky rolled his eyes. We went back in, and he draped his soaked overcoat over the radiator. His cast had turned grey from moisture. I leaned against the doorjamb,

'Should I close the curtains?'

'Maybe you could cut the bullshit and offer me a bowl

of stew? God, is it shitty out there.'

I went to the kitchen and heated up the goulash. When I came back, Slibulsky sat leaning forward in my chair, following the game through his dark shades. I handed him the plate and sat next to him on the armrest.

'What's the score?'

'First set for us.'

We spooned goulash into our mouths for a while. As the Swede was serving in the fourth game, Slibulsky set his plate aside, wiped his mouth and said: 'Pretty vile stuff. By the way – I know the name of that guy.'

I set my spoon back on the plate.

'Boy, you're really building suspense – should I wait to serve the dessert while you proceed with further revelations?'

'Come off it. It's useless information in any case. The guy was put behind bars two weeks ago for receiving stolen goods. Name's Mario Beckmann.'

'Is that info from Charlie?'

'No, from a guy at the Queen of Hearts.'

We stared at each other briefly. Then I shrugged. 'Probably wouldn't have been any use to me anyway. I'm pretty sure it's a gang of forgers.'

I took the plates back to the kitchen. Slibulsky shouted:

'What's your next move?'

'Got a tip. A villa in Gellersheim.'

'Where?'

'Gellersheim!'

I put the saucepan in the refrigerator. Winding things up, McEnroe smashed an overhead ball and made the break. Slibulsky growled his appreciation. I waited for the first serve – fifteen love. Then I took a fresh shirt out of the closet and kicked my shoes under the bed.

'And how do you like being a snooper?'

After a moment's silence, he growled back from the chair: 'Kayankaya, do you know what makes you such an exceptional detective? It's your ability to stay stuck for weeks on the same thing…'

Ten minutes later I had shaved and changed clothes. I stepped out of the bathroom, picked the mail off the bed, and sat on the armrest again. Slibulsky had stretched out his legs and sat there with his arms crossed over his chest, slightly hampered in that pose by his plaster cast. Now the score was five three.

'You don't know what you missed.' Without turning his gaze away from the screen, Slibulsky waved his left arm. 'He's at the net, he's made two returns, the ball comes down the line, he has to jump, and then – he just smashes it back, in mid-air!'

I lit a cigarette and thumbed through the mail: phone bill, power bill, a letter from the building management, stacks of advertisements, and then suddenly the handwritten note. It was awkwardly penned on a sheet from an Interconti Frankfurt hotel note pad: 'The girl is in Dietzenbach, at After Hours.' I stared at it, not sure what to think. Then I handed it to Slibulsky: 'You know the joint?'

A pause.

'I think it's a brothel for queers.' He looked up. 'What would they want a girl for?'

'I have no idea. But someone must have had one.'

Slibulsky scratched his neck. 'If even the queers are

69

muscling in on this trade in women – then things are getting really weird.'

Match point McEnroe. Loud yelling. 'Quiet, please' – an ace, with the look that indicates he finds it hard to believe he has to deal with such a low-grade opponent.

I got up and took my Beretta from the shelf. 'The next game is Becker against Carl Arsch. But I have to go now.'

'To Gellersheim?'

'No, to Dietzenbach.'

I put in the clip. Slibulsky reached for the remote control.

'If someone calls?'

'Get their name and number and tell them I'll call back tomorrow. There's beer in the icebox.'

On my way down I ran into Mr Knapp. He studied biology, owned a car plastered with campground stickers from all over the world and equipped with a removable tape player, which he carried around everywhere, as well as a girlfriend who also was a biology student. This time he was carrying the tape player and a cordovan briefcase with a combination lock. His outfit was beige. Even his green jacket was beige, somehow. He would probably look beige even if he wore a black suit with red polka dots.

As always, he greeted me cordially: 'Guten Tag.' As never before, I replied: 'Heil Hitler!'

Totally confused, wildly waving his briefcase and tape player, he stopped and stuttered. 'Wha – what did you say?'

'Didn't you sign that petition? For the Republikaner billboard?'

'But...,' he shook his head in protest, 'I didn't do it because I support their aims – on the contrary. In fact, I am an outspoken – how should I put it...' He opened and shut his mouth a couple of times, searching for the word. 'Friend of foreigners.' He nodded and beamed.

'If I'm included in that,' I said, 'you better watch out that this friend doesn't punch you in the nose.'

'Please don't say that, Mr Kayankaya. I signed only because I think it is important to give everyone a chance to voice his opinion freely – this is a democracy, after all.'

'Right. Even when there are times when it seems as if that freedom of expression had been reserved only for Republicans – and people who have no opinion – it is still available to others. And on that note, Mr Knapp,' I raised my right arm, 'break a leg!'

Chapter 7

'You're my baby, baby, baby – oh yeah. You're my
sunshine, sunshine, sunshine – oh yeah. You're my –'
krzzzzzzfghtntrzzzzzz '– the Chancellor put on a hat in
honour of the Jewish victims of National Socialism.
President Richard von Weizsacker, who also attended the
ceremony, concluded his speech by asking, aren't we all
human beings, after all? And I agree wholeheartedly: Yes!
Yes, we are human beings. The weather –'
krzzzzzzzerbgmgnzzzzzz '– in the light of stars far away, I
love you night and day, as if we were two stars, shining
there so fa–' krzzzzzzzzfghnlrtzzzzzzz '– now a purely
technical question, Mr Fips. How do you manage to
concentrate on your text while simultaneously trying to
beat a hole into the table top with your forehead? Just
considering the rhythmical –' 'In my heart lives a machine
gun, and my texts are bursts fired into the dark future.' 'I
see, well, that's nicely put. But you haven't answered my
question. Could you tell us something about the visual

aspect – what do you do when blood starts running into your eyes? Do you wear sweatbands on your wrists, like a tennis player, or does it just fly off to the side?' 'In my heart lives a machine gun, and my words are bursts into the dark future – if you like, I can read a poetic sequence that will answer your question.' 'Uh – well, why not. But please let's not have any blood stains on the carpeting –' krzzzzzzfgnerzzzz '– the President's speech yesterday, on the theme Joy through Peace, at the beginning of the NATO exercise Friendly Touch, met with both national and international acclaim…'

I turned it off. I thought that I would have liked to work for the radio. It is a medium in sore need of improvement, and I know hardly anyone who has not at least a hundred times, behind the wheel or the shop counter, thought about what a good radio programme might sound like. But people who work for radio stations probably think the same thing. They sit there at their turntables, put on 'Tommy and His Jolly Bavarian Brass,' and think they'd like to work for the radio.

Fifteen miles later I passed the sign that told me I had entered Dietzenbach. I parked the Opel, got out, and looked around. A bird, a distant moped, and somewhere else a lawnmower. It seemed as if the inhabitants were busy laying their town to rest. The corpse was laid out before me: sparkling windows with drawn curtains, shiny mailboxes, manicured front yards, disinfected pavements. The parked cars looked as if they had just been removed from their Styrofoam packaging. I liked small German towns. They made me think that I had made a few good decisions: rush-hour traffic, winter sales, noisy neighbours, even the construction work on the expansion of the Frankfurt subway that had been going on right under my window – in a place like Dietzenbach, all those things now appeared in a much kinder light.

I walked fifty yards down the street, up to a 'rustic' fence and a man who was cleaning the licence plate of his BMW with a toothbrush.

'Good afternoon.'

The guy looked up and assumed the expression they all do when they stand in their front yard next to their automobile behind their 'rustic' fences and assume that another person might have less than or nothing like what they have. Waving the toothbrush he approached me: 'No need nothing, no buy nothing!'

'Is it caries, or does his breath just smell bad?'

'What smells bad here?'

He stopped in front of me, shoulders back, chin jutting.

'Your friend over there. The one with the rubber feet and the pipe up his ass.'

He turned, then turned back, looking irritated. Flexing his right arm like a weightlifter, he repeated: 'No need nothing, no buy nothing.' When I still didn't make a move to leave, he said it a third time, roaring on behalf of the town of Dietzenbach: 'No need nothing, no buy nothing!'

'Very good. Now we know that one. Let's move on to Lesson Number Two: How do I get to the After Hours club? And let's be a little more on the ball if you don't mind.'

He froze in the middle of a motion that could have led to all sorts of things. Slowly, setting one foot behind the other, he backed off in the direction of his BMW.

'Fuck off! Get the hell outta here!' His voice turned falsetto. 'I sure hope I didn't catch anything from talking to you, you –'

I held up my right hand and imitated the motion of a windscreen wiper while pulling a scrap of paper out of my trousers pocket with my left. 'Number seventeen Hirschgraben. Tell me how to get there, or I'll spit on your tulips.'

Pale, and holding the toothbrush like a crucifix in front of his chest, he leaned back against the radiator. 'Go straight, then right at the second traffic light, and you'll see a pink neon sign…'

'Much obliged.' I waved. 'And keep on studying your German. There are times, these days, when the place feels like a foreign country.'

A heavy, dark brown, wooden door with a one-way peephole; to the left of it, a menu of drinks, to the right a brass plate with a marble bell button. I pressed it, and a taped voice croaked: 'Please wait; attendez s'il vous plaît; bitte warten!' Minutes later, the door opened, and a pale runt with facial hair and large eyes clung to the frame. White tennis shoes, jeans, an opalescent shirt open to the navel, a gold chain, and a quart of pomade in his hair.

'What can I do for you?'

'I'd like to speak to your boss.'

His long thin fingers beat a nervous tattoo on the doorframe.

'Sorry, but Gerhard is not available at the moment.'

'Is he here?'

'I told you, he's not available.'

Before he could close the door again, I pushed him aside and entered the bar. It stank of alcohol and brimming ashtrays. The chairs had been put up on the tables among many glasses that were empty except for straws and bits of fruit. In the back of the room there was a cabaret stage. On it stood the remains of a gigantic pink cake, and next to it lay an unshaven fatso dressed in sexy lingerie. Two neon tubes cast their sallow light on the scene. In addition to the entrance, there were three more doors in the room. All three had signs on them: 'Pool', 'Safety First', and 'Private.'

Someone was tugging at my jacket. 'What do you think you're doing? Get out of here!'

I turned and grabbed the runt's shirt collar. He tried to hit me, but I held him at arm's length. I pointed at the fat guy.

'Is that Gerhard?'

No reaction. Now he was completely motionless. He stared straight ahead and seemed determined to keep his mouth shut.

'Listen, kiddo, tell me where your boss is, or I'll glue you to the ceiling.'

A quick tremor ran through his body, but that was all. He hung his head as if resigned to be glued to the ceiling for Gerhard's sake. I let him go, went to the door marked 'Private'. A cast-iron spiral staircase took me to the hallway of the second floor. Another set of three doors. I picked the one behind which I could hear quiet radio music. I pushed it and was surprised by sunlight. The near-darkness in the bar and hall had made me forget it was still day. It was a fully furnished office with a computer, fax machine, an array of telephones, lamps, screens. The third surprise was Gerhard himself, or rather, the click of the safety catch on his gun.

'Hands up, sweetheart.'

I raised my arms and turned slowly. He was tall, wide, and well fed. Perhaps a little too tall, wide, and well fed. Steely blue eyes stared at me out of a salon-tanned face framed by a marcelled, peroxide-blond mane. A bit like Kalli Feldkamp in leather. His feet were encased in athletic shoes adorned with American flags.

'My, my,' he rolled his eyes, 'a genuine sheikh.'

I responded with a tired grin. 'Can I put my arms down now?'

'But why? You look good that way.'

Holding the gun, he minced around me. Facing me again, he smacked his lips loudly. I stared at the ceiling.

'Cute, really cute… Your beer belly needs a little work, and that haircut needs modernising. In some nice threads – well, you wouldn't be a Don Johnson exactly, but chubby fellows have their own kind of charm. Right?'

'My arms are falling asleep.'

'Just keep them up there, sweetheart. As long as it's just your arms…' He winked, sat down behind the desk and put his feet up on it. 'You just have to *emphasise* your type a little more.'

'And what would that be? A cross between Gerd Muller and Ghaddafi?'

He groaned with delight. 'Ghaddawi! My idol!' His eyelids drooped. 'With him, I could do a thousand and one nights – at least.' He tilted his head to the side. 'But in your shoes, I'd go for the more rustic look. Navy blue, sleeves rolled up, heavy boots – you're the sailor type.'

'I'll keep it in mind. But right now I'm looking for a woman by the name of Sri Dao Rakdee. I've been told she's staying here.'

He gave a start. 'A woman…?' He made a face as if the devil had just run past. Then he brightened and flashed his capped teeth at me.

'Oh, you must mean Dolores, our transy? But she isn't here today.'

'No, I don't mean Dolores. I mean – fuck you.'

I let my arms drop and pulled out my cigarettes. Dumbfounded, he watched as I lit one, shook the match out and tossed it into his pencil holder.

'So? You going to shoot me just because I entered your office without knocking? I'm here because I'm looking for that woman – and she can't help being born a woman, can she? Now tell me if there's someone of her gender in this joint.'

Very slowly, he took his feet off the desk, sat up straight, and held the gun with both hands aiming it at my forehead. His eyes, glittering a moment ago, were dry and cold. His voice had an edge to it.

'You're not a cop, are you?'

'Do I look like one?'

'You look like a boozy little rat.'

The sky had darkened, and there was a distant sound of thunder. My quota of half-assed loudmouths was filled for the day.

I pointed at his nose. 'Booger.'

He didn't get it right away. Then, in a reflex motion, his

hand rose to his face, and he glanced down. My first blow made him drop the gun, the second did some damage to his tanned jaw, and the third made him gasp for air.

I picked up the gun and sat down on the edge of the desk. 'All right, let's take it from the top. Is that woman here?'

Bent over in his chair, holding his jaw with one hand and his stomach with the other, he looked at me in disbelief. Then he shook his head, cautiously, and groaned: 'You're out of your mind.'

'Yes or no will do just fine. Are you a dealer in forged papers?'

'Forged papers?' He let go of his jaw and waved at the high tech scenery. 'I make half a million a year just on the stock exchange. Why would I deal in shit like that?'

'But you seemed pretty concerned when it occurred to you that I might be a cop.'

'So? I just don't like you guys. Can't help it. Besides, you have no right whatsoever to barge in here. That business was three years ago. This is a completely clean shop. We don't even show dubious videos.'

'What business?'

'Oh, stop pretending. The one about the kid who wasn't sixteen yet, whatever – the fucking little liar…'

His face brightened in mid-sentence. While I was still wondering what had cheered him up so suddenly, I was struck by a lightning bolt, straight down the spine to the tips of my toes. With a glaring light in my head and the feeling of falling into the void I heard his voice from far away: 'Come here, angel, let me give you a kiss for that.'

I was rushing down an endless steep slope at an infernal

pace. No one and nothing could have stopped me, not even I myself. Everything was white. No sky, no sun, no trees. Just white. The skis carried me across the snow at such speed that I had no time to breathe. I had no poles. I went down, ever farther down, my heart slid into my head. But suddenly nothing was white any more, everything turned black, and a huge abyss yawned at the end. I was unable to stop, my body was bereft of all sensation, and a deafening noise spread out over everything, the roar of a thousand firestorms.

I opened my eyes. About a foot away, a vacuum cleaner was moving back and forth. Behind it, working the vac with one hand and holding a gun in the other, was the runt. He looked at me with sad big eyes. I tried to move my head. It felt as if someone had stuck a knife into my neck. I sat up, gingerly. They had swept me into a corner of the bar. The dirty glasses were gone, the chairs were back on the floor, and the place smelled of violets. The vacuum curved around my feet. I closed my eyes tight.

'Isn't it neat enough now? Or are you expecting a visit from your Mum?'

He kept pushing the monster around the floor. Then he hissed at me: 'Fuck off. I'm doing my job.'

He waved the gun in the direction of the door. I managed a painful nod.

'All right, all right.'

I was sure that I wasn't the first to poke fun at him; nor would I be the last. I could imagine heavy-duty leather guys like Gerhard stomping on him every day. One day he would probably kill one of them, and he would certainly get caught. In the joint, people would start stomping on him again, and so on and so forth, all the way to the coffin. 'You won't have me to stomp on any more' is what they should engrave on his headstone. If he'd get a headstone.

Five minutes later I was up on my feet. I touched the matted spot on the back of my head.

'You've got some real strength in those arms, kiddo.'

'Fuck off.'

I sighed, tapped my forehead, and staggered to the bar. My head, my stomach, all my franchised parts clamoured for a drink. Without asking for permission, I grabbed a bottle of scotch and raised it to my lips. Some time later, when I set it down, the knife in my neck had turned to a rubber arrow. The fat guy in lingerie was sitting at the other end of the counter. He stared dimly in my direction, then raised his hand and waved furtively: 'Care to join me in a drink?'

I twinkled back. 'Sorry, but I've got the curse.' I staggered out into the rain.

'Gina?'

'Yes.'

'It's Kayankaya.'

She laughed, and we exchanged a few pleasantries about a mutual female friend with whom they had spent the previous evening. That person must have gossiped quite extensively about my alleged mating behaviour. Gina and Slibulsky had been living together for more than seven years, and apart from occasional tussles, they got along famously, although they were a rather incongruous couple:

Gina, a young thirty, studied archeology, saved seals, read fat books, and worked as a teacher in a dance and deportment school for girls from good families. She claimed that this was just a job to pay the rent, but I wasn't always so sure. One memorable evening she explained to me how napkins had to be folded, and why. On the other hand, she was as unconcerned about Slibulsky's lifestyle as she was about whether other people were as interested in old postcards as she was.

'Listen, Gina; Slibulsky told me he broke his arm because he fell downstairs. Do you happen to know what stairs?'

'In the whorehouse, of course.'

'That's all he told you?'

'That's all.'

'Mhm. And that legacy from the aunt in Berlin – what do you know about that?'

'What's to know? He used it to pay off his debts. Why do you ask?'

'Oh, no particular reason.'

The rain sounded like a shower of golf balls against the glass walls of the phone booth. Around the booth, a small lake was forming.

'No, you see, I'm recommending him to my tax accountant, and the guy needs to know a few things about him… What kinds of debts were they?'

She made a pert puffing noise. 'Just debts.'

'How much did he inherit?'

'Fifty thou.'

Now it was my turn to puff. 'When did he get the money?'

'In January. But they withheld the tax before it was paid.'

'I see – well, then, I don't suppose my accountant will be interested in that. Thanks, Gina, and let's keep this to ourselves, OK? I want to make Slibulsky a present of a free advice session with my guy.'

'Gee, you must be rolling in it.'

'Well, at the moment… Talk to you soon.'

The sky was turning even darker. I stared into space for a while. Then I tore the door open and bounded across the puddles to my car. Mrs Olga may have been an alarmist, but she did not hallucinate things.

Chapter 8

Shortly after five-thirty I drove into Gellersheim. Ten minutes later I had located Rosenacker, a short street on the outskirts. It looked as if a couple of nouveau riches had decided to emulate the truly wealthy. The nameplates on the gates were too big, the driveways too small, and every villa looked different: some were perfectly round, others had Gothic arches or Bavarian-style carved wood curlicues. In front of an aerodynamic one-storey building stood a gigantic flagpole: the flag bore the legend Theo Manz Cinema Production. A closer look revealed that the flag was plastic and that the garden gate had no handles. I was reminded of a movie type who had hired me to follow his future wife around for a week. He wanted to know if she was likely to waste his money in boutiques and bookshops. At the end of the assignment, he was unable to pay me because one of his projects had just collapsed. He told me that I should, nevertheless, be grateful for having made his acquaintance: he would gladly arrange a small part for me in his next movie. When I told him I didn't want a part in a movie, only my fee, he said he was 'somehow quite totally amazed,' as he put it. In style of speech and dress, this forty-year-old owner of a Volvo and a penthouse had an insatiable desire to give the impression of a high school student hitchhiking to the south. My fee arrived in dribs and drabs, a hundred marks a shot, at intervals corresponding to the times I saw him dining on red snapper and drinking bubbly in fashionable restaurants.

In its surroundings, Number Six looked pleasantly normal. The two-storey brick box with a vine-covered terrace stood in a large well-kept garden with a pond and two driveways: one was hidden behind dog rose bushes, for staff and deliveries, the other was covered with light-coloured gravel and bordered by roses and cast-iron carriage lights mounted on poles. Through the bars of the black iron gate I could see tyre tracks. These were the only signs that anyone except for the gardener had been visiting here for a while. All the shutters were closed, the mailbox was full of advertising materials, and the moist glittering lawn looked undisturbed. I regretted that the thunderstorm was over. In the present radiant sunlight I had the unpleasant feeling of having my every move observed from a long way off. Nothing could remain hidden from Mrs Olga whose neighbouring villa with its little pink turrets looked like an American miniature copy of Heidelberg Castle.

The name on the mailbox was 'Dr Schelling.' I acted as if I had stopped at the wrong number and walked down the street past the staff entrance. After ten steps or so, I turned, ran back, jumped over the wooden fence and landed on a wire. Held up by plastic supports about three feet above ground it stretched all around the walls of the plot, ending in small grey boxes installed in the corners. I got up and took cover behind the nearest tree. Nothing happened. The alarm must have been turned off. Hunched over, I ran across flowerbeds, overturned a few pieces of garden furniture, reached the terrace, and pressed myself against the glass sliding door. Shielding my eyes with my hands I scanned the room inside and saw a couch, some chairs, a television set. As I slid to one side, the door slid open as well, to my surprise. After casting a quick glance all around, I went in.

Instead of the usual cold stale smell of furniture in vacant houses, I noticed an odour of stale cooking, with a lemony whiff of men's perfume thrown in. I listened. A wall clock was ticking, a refrigerator humming somewhere in the distance. I touched the radiator. It had been turned off but was still warm. Then I noticed what I hadn't been able to see from outside: the light was on in the entrance hall. I proceeded cautiously to the door, leaned against the doorframe, pulled my Beretta. Moving past a built-in kitchen and a toilet I reached the stairs. Halfway up the stairs I noticed, diagonally below me, a basement door. I tiptoed back, slipped the safety catch, and went down the steps to a large room furnished with a football game machine, a pinball machine, and a ten-metre-long dining table. On the table stood a huge tin bucket in the midst of some thirty plates with remnants of stew and bread on them. There was silverware on the floor, several chairs had been overturned; there were three more games on the pinball machine, and there was a ball in the chute. I walked across the room toward a curtain of grey blanket material. I pushed it aside and found myself in a narrow, yellow-lit hallway with doors to the right and the left. Each one of the rooms was some twenty-five square feet in size and furnished with three army cots, a sink, and the kind of light fixture you find in garages. Only the last room on the left contained something else.

He lay on his stomach, stripped down to his socks, and the grey skin on his arms was tattooed with images of women and weapons. He looked surprised. Under the moustache, his mouth was open, as if he wanted to say 'But –?' or something like that. But he wasn't saying anything, and he would never say anything again. His neck was broken.

I felt his pulse, then covered him with a blanket. I went through his clothes which lay scattered on the floor. There was no wallet or address book, only a box of matches, half a pack of cigarettes, and a nine-millimetre Browning pistol. I slipped the gun in my pocket, pulled the blanket off him again, and read the inscriptions on his arms: 'Manne loves Ingrid'; 'Manne loves Sabine'; 'Manne loves Iris more than all the chicks before!'; and 'Manne hates Tempo Hundred!' No last name. I sat down next to him and smoked two cigarettes. Then I went out into the garden behind the house, found a tool shed, took a shovel and dug a three-foot-deep pit next to a basement window. Then I took the cable of the electric lawnmower and went back to Manne. After I had wrapped him and his clothes into a huge sausage, I pulled him to the window and heaved and pushed him outside. A little later,

I had covered the shallow grave so that it was invisible to the casual eye.

Then I checked out the house. I went through cupboards, chests, desks, nightstands, I even looked under the rugs, but didn't come up with anything. Except for the basement, the house was like an empty furniture showroom. There were no letters, no books, there wasn't even an old toothbrush. Only that stew and Manne, and a heap of vegetable scraps in the kitchen garbage can.

I found a telephone and called Gellersheim information for Dr Schelling's number. It wasn't listed. No Dr Schelling in Frankfurt, Offenbach, Mainz, Wiesbaden, or Kassel, either. After I hung up, I remembered the shovel. I took it back to the tool shed. As I stepped out of the shed, I saw a note pinned to the wall with a pair of garden shears. It said: 'Water lilies? New gravel? Trim trees – new ladder!' And there was a phone number.

It rang three times. Then came a cool, businesslike male voice: 'Olschewski for Schmitz.'

'Schmitz?'

'Eberhard Schmitz. I am his secretary. What can I do for you?'

'Well, I... You mean Eberhard Schmitz, Georg's brother?'

'That's correct.'

'...'

'Hello?'

'Yes, yes, I'm still here... I wanted to know – see, I'm the gardener at the villa in Gellersheim, and for the trees I need a new ladder – to trim them, you see.'

'Buy one and add it to the invoice.'

'Many thanks.'

'Anything else?'

I cleared my throat. 'Well, maybe you could ask the parties who come here from time to time not to walk all over the fresh flowerbeds…'

'You know you don't have to worry about that. We're paying you enough to make it worth your while to redo the flowerbeds.'

'I just meant –'

'Don't mean, just do your work. Goodbye.'

On the drive back I contemplated the best plan of action and arrived at half a decision. Back in Frankfurt I parked in front of the first tavern with a Henninger sign and walked into a dark booze grotto full of stale tobacco smoke. Two guys in their mid-thirties sat at the bar in their cheap Sunday best. They had half-empty drinks in front of them, hand-rolled cigarettes between their fingers. Behind the counter a girl was drying dishes. The proprietor sat reading an illustrated magazine. There was no one else in the joint. Lit-up slot machines stood by the wall, old carnival garlands hung above the tables. The four people turned to look at me. Expressionless, pale, flat faces. The proprietor put his magazine away and crossed his arms.

'Private party.'

Faint smiles on the faces of the guys at the bar. I rammed both hands in my trousers pockets and looked at the floor.

'Let's keep this sweet and short. This is a public place,

and I would like to have a beer and make a phone call. But if it so happens that this is a private party, or that the beer taps have been turned off, or that you're closing this very second – then I'll be back. Every day. And I'll bring some friends. Big friends, sensitive friends, friends with baseball bats. We'll make this joint our neighbourhood pub. So you better see about getting some Turkish music, and I don't think there'll be much of a demand for your pork chops.'

'All right, all right.'

The proprietor made a resigned gesture. Then he nodded to the girl and returned to his magazine. Disappointed, the guys in their mid-thirties concentrated on their drinks.

'And where is your phone?'

The proprietor took his time. Then he looked up and said: 'We don't have one. We use smoke signals.'

Was that ever a riot. The guys at the bar almost fell off their stools, and the proprietor had to wipe tears from his eyes. While the three kept on erupting into renewed guffaws, the girl put a phone on the counter and pushed it toward me, flashing me an embarrassed smile under cover of the beer taps. After the wild merriment subsided, I dialled Slibulsky's and Gina's number. I let it ring for a long time. Then I hung up and received my beer. I sucked it down in one go, nodded to the girl, and walked to the door. A roar came just as I grabbed the doorknob: 'Hey, you haven't paid!' I opened the door.

'I'll send you a buffalo hide by the end of the week. That should pay for the beer.'

Chapter 9

'Come on, come on, try it, double your money – keep your eye on it and win! Where's the ball? Here? No. Here? No. Here it is! Let's keep going – a hundred marks on the table, no tricks, no double bottom – this is an honest game. Keep your eye on it…'

The small white ball skittered from left to right, up and down, bounced off the pavement, reappeared sometimes between his fingers, sometimes under one of the three matchboxes, and finally disappeared. Once more he switched the boxes around, stopped, waved a wad of hundred-mark bills in the air and looked around with an innocent expression.

'Where's the ball?'

He had been kneeling on the pavement for ten minutes, whirling things around, and had taken two intoxicated Japanese and a small-town loudmouth in a deerskin outfit for four hundred marks. Twenty or so male heads waved sceptically in the April wind. All of them knew it was impossible to win, but all of them kept staring at his wad of bills.

The wind gusted heavily, cars honked, people ran, and a loudspeaker voice proclaimed a revolution in the realm of dishwashing brushes, but silence reigned in the circle around the shell game guy. After he clapped his hands and got ready to rattle off his spiel again, a Pole took two steps forward, placed a boot on the box to the left, extracted a hundred-mark bill from his wallet, and said: 'Show.'

The men in the circle came alive; some of them nodded approval, some turned away, shaking their heads.

The man contemplated the boot. 'Do I look like a shoeshine boy?'

The Pole shrugged and bent down. But just as he was about to pick up the box, a short fat guy stumbled out of the void, uttered some drunken babble, and knocked him over. A loud murmur rose from the audience, and before the Pole had got up, cursing, and brushed off his trousers, and the other guy had vanished again, the ball had changed places.

I leaned against the display window of a sex shop, smoked a cigarette, and studied the entrance to the Eros-Centre Elbestrasse.

It was almost six o'clock. The street vendors were packing up their wares.

Just as the Pole got ready to punch out the con man, the plastic door-flaps flew open and Slibulsky came bouncing down the stairs. I waited until he had reached the crossing. Just as I tossed my cigarette away, the Pole came crashing into my side. I fell down on the pavement, he fell on top of me, and both of us ended up in the gutter. He was groaning and not making any attempt to get off of me. They must have punched him with a knuckle-duster. One of his incisors was gone, and his mouth was spraying blood like a leaky hose. I pushed him aside, got to my feet, and looked around. Slibulsky had disappeared.

'Sorry, but how could I know that the Pollack would lose his cool that way?' He was a member of the shell game gang; not yet eighteen, milky skin, an old man's pouches under his eyes. He, too, had made a bet, but he had won. A decoy. Now he shifted his weight from one leg to the other, rubbed his ironclad fist, and waited for my reaction. Maybe he thought I was one of the boys of the red-light district it's better not to mess with. 'But I am sorry, 'cause of your suit, I mean.'

I checked and noted that I did, indeed, look as if I had just come from a butchering party.

'Yeah, that'll be some dry cleaning bill…'

He retreated a step. 'Yeah, well –'

'But maybe we can settle this some other way. I'm sure you know Ernst Slibulsky, the guy who works over there at the centre?'

'The guy with the lumpy nose?'

'That's him. He's got a broken arm. I'd like to know where that happened.'

'Where he broke his arm? No idea. I just run into him once in a while. And I hear people talk.'

'And where do you run into him?'

'Around here. He's always in and out of there, and sometimes he's over there in The Die.'

'Ah –'

'Hey, man, you're not a cop, are you?'

I looked up and shrugged. 'Something like that.'

Looking as if he had stepped on something, he said 'Shit!' He ran over to his buddies and gave them the scram sign. Within two seconds, the shell game arena was empty.

In the meantime, the Pole had managed to sit up. He leaned against a car tyre and patted his lips with a corner of his shirt.

I lit a cigarette and stuck it between his fingers. He nodded absentmindedly. That was his only reaction. Maybe he didn't smoke. I slapped him on the shoulder, mumbled a few encouraging words, and crossed the street.

The Smiling Die should really have been called 'The Smiling Chinese.' The probability of a smiling die was as unlikely as the probability of an unsmiling Mr Wang. No matter if men who had lost everything crawled weeping to his doorstep, the police conducted a raid, or the Mafia broke every fixture in the place – the small man from Hong Kong sat behind the counter, his arms crossed over his chest, and smiled as if the world were one big spring roll. At the time it was said that he was abroad. Two months ago, someone had strangled Mrs Wang and tossed a young fellow and a wardrobe out of her bedroom window on the fourth floor. Since then, Mr Wang's bodyguard was in charge of business. Schlumpi, or 'Ass-with-Ears' Peter, never smiled. Even if he had smiled, no one would have noticed: after a car racing accident, the skin on the lower half of his face had been replaced by a graft from his backside.

The two small rooms and bar were down in the basement. They were furnished with tables for roulette, blackjack, and craps, chessboards and timers. The joint, once elegant, had come down in the world. Everything was ramshackle and stained, even the dealer. He was wearing a dark suit and a bow tie, but a button was missing on his shirt, and his cuffs were frayed. Narrow windows permitted a view of high heels ambling back and forth. Eleven guys were sitting around the roulette table, drinking beer and losing money. I stood at the bar, drinking beer and waiting. The woman behind the counter kept glancing at my suit with a mildly horrified look but did not say anything. No one said anything except for the dealer.

Ten minutes later a door next to the bar, marked 'Office', opened and Schlumpi, wearing a white wolf fur coat, stepped behind the cash register. After he had tossed in a bundle of bills and closed the drawer, he looked up and remarked, after a brief pause:

'What do you know, it's the Robin Hood of Istanbul.'

The door opened again, and Slibulsky came out with a man I didn't know. Slibulsky gave a start. 'Kayankaya – what are you doing here?'

'Having a beer, and listening to Schlumpi's old jokes.'

'Oh…'

While Slibulsky took his leave from the guy I didn't know, Schlumpi leaned on the counter, pointed at my suit, and whispered through his scarred and lipless hole of a mouth: 'Here's another joke – brand new: Kayankaya's been giving head to a cunt on the rag.'

'Incredibly funny. But the funniest thing about it is –'

Slibulsky tugged at my sleeve. 'Come on, let's go.' And to the woman behind the bar: 'Put his beer on my tab.'

The woman nodded.

'Didn't know you knew Schlumpi.'

'And I didn't know you played roulette.'

We crossed Kaiserstrasse in the direction of the railway station. The sun was setting behind the triple arch, and scraps of afterglow lingered to the right and the left. There was a whiff of spring in the air.

'Who told you I was there?'

'A guy in the street.'

We made our way past a bunch of junkies who were attempting a choral version of 'We Are the World' while someone played it on a comb.

'I just wanted to ask you where you broke that arm.'

Slibulsky stopped. 'You were looking for me to ask me that?'

I nodded. He opened his mouth, closed it with a sigh, then opened it again and said: 'In the Centre.'

'Where exactly?'

'Hey, what's the matter with you?'

I tilted my jaw in the direction of the nearest tavern. 'Let's have a beer.'

'I can't. I have to go to work.'

'How about later?'

'Not today, not tomorrow. We're getting some new women in.' He checked his watch. 'I should have been there quite some time ago.'

'All right. But if nothing else, tell me how the game went.'

'What game?'

'Becker against –'

'Oh, that… I didn't watch it to the end. But someone called. Guy called – something to do with trees… Baum?'

'Weidenbusch?'

'Possible. Says it's urgent. Later.'

Just as Slibulsky disappeared in the crowd, an elderly gentleman wearing a red velvet bow tie appeared in front of me and flashed the inside of his waistcoat with its assortment of wristwatches. 'Genuine Swiss watches, Monsieur.'

I bought a particularly ostentatious one, went into a bar and asked for a beer and a corkscrew. Then I lit a cigarette. How deep should the shit get that Slibulsky had got himself into before I would decide not to help him crawl back out of it? I was still pondering that when the waiter came back with my order. He was a small fat fellow with greasy hair combed straight back and an equally greasy apron. After he had taken my money, he pointed at the corkscrew and asked me morosely: 'You going to clean your fingernails with it?'

I shook my head. 'I want to scratch a dedication into the back of a watch.'

'Oh, I see… Well, I was just thinking, I clean mine with it all the time, and we've only got one of them here, and I wouldn't really like it if other people –'

'Not to worry.'

He growled, 'Never mind me, I'm a little strange in some ways,' and disappeared. I looked at my beer. It looked quite normal, really, but I pushed it aside and proceeded to scratch FOR MANNE into the back plate of the watch.

A little later I left the bar and drove home to change clothes.

Chapter 10

The voice on the intercom said: 'Who is there, please?'

'The gardener from Gellersheim.'

'Who, please?'

I repeated my phrase and was told to wait. Minutes passed, then the voice returned: 'With whom do you wish to speak?'

'Mr Schmitz.'

'Sorry, but Mr Schmitz isn't here.'

'His secretary?'

'Mr Olschewski isn't here, either.'

'Did you take a good look?'

'Excuse me?'

On the third floor of the fortress-like building a light went out and a curtain moved.

'Please inform the absent gentlemen that if they don't become present in one minute, I'll tell the police what I found while planting bulbs.'

'And what was that, if I may ask?'

'A watch.'

'Just a moment, please.'

A Jaguar slid up the hill, driving on its parking lights, and disappeared a hundred yards farther up in a small cypress grove. In the moonlit night, the outlines of the treetops looked like cutouts against the sky. I could just make out a watchman's hut. Looking in the other direction, there was a view of Frankfurt, a gigantic lit-up birthday cake twenty miles away. Up here it suddenly felt comforting to be an inhabitant of that cake.

I had lit a cigarette and smoked half of it when the intercom crackled on again: 'Are you still there?'

'Yes.'

'I don't think that a watch found in the garden would be of much interest to the absent gentlemen.'

'But it might be if they were told that there was a man attached to that watch.'

'You mean,' he cleared his throat, 'next to the bulbs you were planting?'

'Yes.'

A moment later, he pressed the buzzer, and I proceeded up the paved walk to the front entrance. The massive oak door swung open, and my salt-and-pepper interlocutor bade me enter. 'Please follow me, sir.'

We crossed the entrance hall and walked down a corridor to the library. Books from floor to ceiling on all four walls, four cordovan armchairs on the dark brown parquet floor. Next to each armchair stood a small table with a lamp and an ashtray; in the middle of the room there was a big table with six chairs. Open on the table, next to further ashtrays, lay an old leather-bound tome.

'Have a seat, sir. He'll be with you in a moment.'

He left the room and closed the door. After I had walked along the shelves for a while, I sat down in front of the old tome and read. On the lam from the cops, an old geezer was carrying an unconscious guy through the sewers of Paris. The water reached to his hips, and the ground under his feet was uneven and muddy. Just as he saw the lantern carried by a police sergeant and stopped to squeeze himself close to the wall, a voice behind me said: 'You want to see me?'

I spun around, and there he stood: a small, hollow-cheeked gentleman with thin reddish blond hair and a tic that kept twitching his head to one side every time he spoke, as if a fly had landed on his face. He was wearing a grey three-piece suit with a dark blue ascot and a silver watch chain across his waistcoat. Arms crossed, right foot slightly forward, on his face an expression of calm combativeness, he stood there against the red and brown background of the wall of books looking like a not entirely successful portrait of royalty – Eberhard Schmitz, the king of the railway station district.

Clumsily, I pointed at the book. 'I was reading – very suspenseful…' I nodded.

He smiled. Then he walked around the table, sat down across from me and pulled a silver case from his vest pocket. It opened with a dignified click, and he offered me a selection of various brands of cigarettes. 'Would you like one?'

There was something slightly awesome about his

nervous tic. I picked an unfiltered number of a brand I didn't know. During the subsequent ceremony which consisted of his selecting a cigarette, tapping it against his thumbnail, lighting mine, lighting his, and putting the lighter back in his pocket, the gaze of his yellow eyes never left my face. Finally, he took the cigarette out of his mouth and remarked, with a quick glance at the book: 'I'm glad to see that gardeners are able to appreciate things beyond mowed lawns.'

'Yes, indeed.' I nodded again. 'The only problem is that I'm in no position to tell you what gardeners appreciate.'

'You're saying that you have as much in common with gardeners as I have with persons who do not take action when strangers trespass on their property without permission?'

'That's about it. Even though I don't know whom you're referring to.'

'I'm referring to you.'

'Then I may assume that the people whose tracks I found in Gellersheim were no strangers to you? That they had been lodged there with your consent?'

A pause. He used the ashtray, leaned back and ran his palm across the edge of the table, as if to see how sharp it was.

'Who are you?'

'Kemal Kayankaya, private investigator.'

'Private investigator...' He dragged on his cigarette and disappeared for a moment in a cloud of smoke. 'One of those dirty types who make most of their money through blackmail.'

'There's bad apples in every barrel. Private investigators,

property owners – you name it. I once saw a Salvation Army officer empty a collection box into his own pocket, and –'

He cut me off. 'Let's get down to business.'

I extinguished my cigarette and took the ostentatious watch out of my pocket. I slid it across the table.

'I found it on a dead man. In your house. And there was enough stew left for half a regiment. Tell me where those people are now, and I'll give you time to remove the corpse.'

After he had examined the watch from all sides, he carefully put it back on the table and shook his head.

'That house has stood empty for three years. Only the gardener has a key.'

'That's not what I understood from your secretary.'

'It must have been a misunderstanding.'

'What about the dead man?'

He stressed each word separately: 'That, too, was a misunderstanding.'

'So be it. Guess I'll go to the police, to clarify all the misunderstandings.'

I reached for the watch but he was faster. 'You'll leave that here.'

'You like it that much? I can tell you where you can get one. Quite cheaply, too.'

He ignored me and slipped the watch into his breast pocket, pulling out a chequebook with the same motion. 'You won't go to the police. At this time, I can't afford any publicity, no matter how far-fetched.' While the butt of his cigarette glowed and darkened in the ashtray, and I wondered if he'd really let me off so easily, he made out a cheque for twenty thousand marks.

He handed it to me, and my jaw dropped. 'Holy smoke! It has to be a *major* misunderstanding.'

With a condescending little smile, he put his fountain pen and cheque book back where they belonged, pushed himself away from the table, and stood up. 'I'm used to such affairs, and I know that I can save myself a lot of grief by spending a few dimes. Dimes – you understand?'

I nodded. 'Sure. Dimes.' I folded the cheque. He waited until I had put it in my wallet. Then he pointed at the door. I would have liked to find out the title of the book about the old geezer, but it didn't seem like the right time to ask. As we walked out into the entrance hall he looked almost contented. 'You see – you *are* a blackmailer.'

'You don't want to know why I searched your house? It doesn't interest you at all?'

'No, it doesn't.' We walked a couple of steps.

'What if I go to the police anyway?'

He stopped and looked down at the floor. For several seconds, all that was heard was the sound of our breathing. Finally, he looked at me and said, with a mildly sad tinge to his voice: 'Listen carefully, young man. You better not do that, if you want to cross a street safely in this city, or in this country, or anywhere in the world. I am a peace-loving man – hence that cheque – but a mere hint from me would suffice to wipe you off the face of the earth. In case you haven't quite got the picture: You're talking to Eberhard Schmitz. And who are you? There's a difference. One of the greatest magnitude.'

'For sure.' I nodded, for the last time. 'You may well be right about that.' Then I pointed at his chest. 'But we'll both die of lung cancer.'

Chapter 11

Loaded down with sandwiches, cookies, chocolate, newspapers, a bottle of Scotch, and two bottles of water, I left the main railway station. It was almost ten-thirty at night. I hurried across the square and crossed the first street. At the second crossing I had to stop for a herd of tourist buses. Suddenly a bell rang behind me, and someone screeched hysterically: 'Can't you see? This is a bicycle lane!'

I whipped around and roared: 'Don't you know how to ride that thing? You've got ten yards leeway there.'

The bicyclist braked, turned, and approached me with a stern missionary look on his face. It was a young man in a green-glittering Fifties-style outfit, stiff blow-dried hair, and a T-shirt that said Born to Be Wild.

'This is a bicycle lane. It's for bicycles. I could have knocked you down, and it would have been your fault,' he informed me, nodding to his own words and coming to a stop in front of me. It was obvious that he expected some sign of gratitude or remorse, and it seemed to me that he would have liked to prolong our conversation.

I left him standing and ran across the street to my car. As I passed him a short while later behind the railway station, I was tempted to show him a perfectly legal brake test.

I drove past the convention building and the Plaza Hotel and on to the autobahn, away from the city lights into dark blue night. I passed the time by trying to calculate how long twenty thousand marks would last in some southern clime. If I had kept going, and the Opel had held up, which was unlikely, I could have been sitting under a straw roof on a beach the following morning, enjoying my shrimp and white wine in the company of a waitress and Whitney Houston on the jukebox. I leaned back. It was warm in the car, and the engine was humming almost perfectly. The waitress came to my table and stayed there all the way to the Gellersheim exit.

I stopped by the first phone booth to call Weidenbusch. His phone rang seven times.

'Yes, hello?'

'Kayankaya. Have you abandoned your position?'

'No, no – I was just taking a bath.'

'Well, what's up?'

'What do you mean?'

There was a tremor in his voice. He must have had a hard day, probably sitting next to the phone, stripping his necktie down to individual fibres, chewing on one piece of peppermint candy after another.

'You did call me this afternoon.'

'Oh, yes. I just wanted to know what you had found out.'

'A whole lot. If I'm not totally mistaken, you'll have your girlfriend back soon.'

His 'Really?' sounded more frightened than delighted. I was taken aback. 'Maybe you're not so happy about that?'

'No, no…' There was a moment's silence. Then he took a deep breath and said:

'But, you see, I've been thinking about all of it today. And I've come to the conclusion that it was not a good idea.'

'What wasn't a good idea?'

'Sri Dao and me. There's the language problem, and, and God knows what might come up. Her family, her background – those really are imponderables. Like right now, me having to deal with gangsters.'

'Listen, Weidenbusch, I understand that you're a wreck, but –'

'No, no, it'll be better for us to separate. I also talked it over with my mother…' A pause. I looked around for the herd of wild horses that I felt galloping over my prone body. There was the sound of paper rustling at the other end of the line.

'In any case, I've decided to pay you for four working days and a per diem of three hundred, that's eleven hundred altogether. If you subtract the five hundred I gave you this morning, I owe you six hundred. I'll mail you the cheque, you'll get it by the end of the week.'

'Excellent. But what do I do about your girlfriend?'

'Well, I thought –'

'You thought I'd go home now and see if there's anything good on the tube? Let me tell you what I'm going to do: I'll go on looking for your friend, and when I've found her, I'll slap her around and tell her greetings from Mr Weidenbusch. I'll explain to her that it's in the language of touch, and love, et cetera.'

'Please don't be so cynical! This has not been an easy decision for me.'

'You don't say.'

I was about to hang up when he said: 'Wait!' And, after a moment's silence: 'Let me know, in any case. Maybe I'm just a little nervous right now. And promise you won't go to the police – no matter what happens.'

Back in the car, I sat there for a thoughtful moment, jingling my car keys.

I parked the Opel in front of Theo Manz Cinema Production and pushed the seat back. Then I put on a black knitted hat, took out my provisions and the Scotch, and settled down to dinner. The lights were still on at Mrs Olga's, and Theo Manz was throwing a party. A long line of upper middle class vehicles were parked along the curb. Rolling Stones songs roared out of the windows, and from time to time a chorus of female voices screeched along: 'I can't get no satisfaction' and other select passages. Number Six was completely dark. When I was done eating, I opened the Scotch and began my vigil. The brick villa stood diagonally in front of me, and I could see the street in my rearview mirror. No matter whom Eberhard Schmitz sent along to dispose of the corpse, I would not miss him. It occurred to me that I should have asked

Weidenbusch if Larsson had tattoos on his arms.

I took a sip and lit a cigarette. Weidenbusch. Slibulsky. Dietzenbach. Slibulsky, again, and McEnroe. The streetlights went out at midnight. My bottle was down to three quarters. I turned on the radio. Music after midnight, Udo Jürgens on every wavelength: 'Show me the place where everybody gets along…' I turned the radio off. A quarrelling couple came out of the Manz residence, waving their arms, running to their car. The man opened the door for her, almost tearing it off its hinges. 'I said let's go kick the ball around on Saturday! I didn't say anything about balling!'

'Oh, Marita plays football?'

They leaned on the roof of the car on opposite sides, each of their necks stretched out like a chicken's, and yelled the street awake.

'Not Marita, her friend, that stupid serial director!'

'So that's what it's come to: you make a date to play football with a "stupid serial director?"'

'Yes! It so happens that I *wrote* that serial!'

Doors slammed, tyres squealed. The car shot through the intersection at sixty miles an hour.

I took out another cigarette. I began to ask myself if Schmitz had been so sure his cheque had withdrawn me from circulation that he had simply gone to bed. The clock on the dashboard told me it was twelve-thirty. I yawned. The sky was overcast again, and the night was pitch-dark. I had some more Scotch, smoked, and stared at the dark outline of the villa. At some point, the bottle must have slipped out of my grasp.

When I woke up, it was dawn. Someone was knocking

on the car door, and I heard a voice:

' 'scuse me, but I saw your Frankfurt plates – could you, could you give me a ride, maybe? Just to get away from here.'

I needed a moment to remember where I was and what I was doing. I roused myself and saw a slightly bedraggled angel behind the side window. Her make-up was smeared and her hairdo had disintegrated into loose strands that hung down around her face. She was banging on the door with a high-heeled shoe. 'I can pay you for the petrol…' It looked like the party was over.

I looked past her at Schmitz's villa. The first thing I saw was a silver-coloured Toyota jeep standing in the drive. Then I noticed that the lights were on, at ground floor level. I unlocked the door while my new acquaintance mumbled, 'Oh, thank you so much!' I jumped out into the street.

'Sorry, dear. You better look for a cab.'

I was off to a flying start. It was miserably cold, and drizzly rain struck my face. Up over the fence alongside the service entrance, across the alarm wire, from tree to tree and past the terrace – I arrived at the sliding door in no time. The shutters were closed, and I could only see thin streaks of light. I put my ear to the wall. Somewhere there was a faint padding sound. After two or three minutes, the sound approached, took a turn right next to me, and stopped with a muted impact. Then nothing happened for quite a while until a quiet voice spoke: 'Hello? Yes, I've checked everywhere. Nothing. Must've been a hoax. Should I go back to the football field? Maybe they know something about it. The dishes? Wait a minute, I'm not a cleaning woman. Besides, that's Manne's job. Nonsense, he'll show up again. All right, all right, but I'll make Manne pay for this. Later.'

Soon after that the padding resumed, grew fainter, faded away. I straightened my back. I had two choices. If I took my Beretta and went down to the basement and forced the guy whose voice I had heard to take me to the refugees, he would get to see me; even though I wasn't quaking in my shoes, I did not take Schmitz's warning lightly. The less contact I had with his people the better. The second choice was the better one. After all, I was just trying to find that woman; at this point, my ambition did not extend to laying bare the corruption of an entire city.

I snuck back to the Opel. Now it was almost daylight.

I turned off the engine. The party angel was fast asleep in the back seat. I pulled out a blanket from under the passenger seat and covered her up with it. Her features had composed themselves, and she had curled up looking almost contented among the bits of foam rubber bursting out of the seams of the seat, old newspapers, and an oilcan. Hers was the kind of cool beauty one could admire in practically every movie of the past; it has now been replaced by so-called faces with character. Her eyelashes spread over her cheeks like fans, and she wore a string of pearls around her neck. I wouldn't have minded taking her back to Frankfurt. I also didn't mind her sleeping in my car. Before it occurred to me to have any objections against dashing back into the drizzly cold, I faced the dashboard again, sipped a little Scotch, and got out.

FIRST FC GELLERSHEIM was what the faded red letters said on the wall of the clubhouse. Iron bars protected the window of the small dusty room. I saw a row of cheap trophies arrayed on the back wall. I turned and looked across the empty football field. Overturned and rotting wooden benches lay next to the sidelines, the corner flag posts were broken, and a torn goal-net fluttered in the wind. The field had deteriorated to scattered tussocks of grass. I kicked an empty beer bottle across the sand and scanned the surrounding woods. The only sound I heard was a barely audible hum. I attributed it to my own head, crossed the penalty area, and found a muddy road. Soon there was nothing but trees on both sides, with little light filtering down from the treetops. I found myself in a desolate half-darkness, twigs crackling underfoot. I decided that this had not been a good idea and turned back. This time I passed the clubhouse on its rearside which sported the remains of a derelict shack: the former locker room. Half of its roof had caved in and piles of splintered glass lay under the gaping windows. I stopped. No head in the world could generate a hum this loud. This was the hum of a generator. I found it under a lean-to behind the locker room. For whom or what was it generating electricity? The non-existent floodlights? Or the empty lidless freezer next to the club bar counter?

I went back to the field, sat down on the edge of an overturned bench, and lit a cigarette. I had smoked about half of it when, some thirty yards into the woods, two headlights appeared. I took cover.

The silver Toyota jeep stood in front of a concrete wall with a grey steel door. The wall was set into a hillock overgrown with shrubs. I had detected no movement for the last ten minutes.

I was huddling behind a tree, my coat collar turned up, the Beretta in my lap. I regretted my choice of shoes; my feet felt like dead fish. After another ten minutes I decided I'd had enough. Cautiously, my shooting iron at the ready, I ran from one tree to the next until I reached the running board of the jeep.

Brimming ashtrays, dozens of music cassettes, two empty Bacardi bottles, boxing and racing magazines, a dog muzzle, and a box of dog food. A plastic guitar and a heart made out of fabric dangled from the rear-view mirror. A sticker on one of the side windows said Afri-Cola All the Way to the Oder. Suddenly the steel door opened and a white beast with a porcine face slipped outside. I crawled under the jeep, but the creature had noticed me. On short, bowed legs it waddled up, stopped in front of me, and looked at me out of blood-shot eye slits. He looked bored, did not growl, didn't even seem to breathe. He just stood there and stared. Heavy footsteps approached, and a martial voice called out: 'Come on, Rambo!' But Rambo didn't come. Rambo kept his eyes on me and yawned. This caused his head to split into two halves and show a whole army of small white teeth, shiny as knife points.

'Rambo!' The footsteps grew fainter. Rambo stayed where he was. In slow motion I tried to raise the Beretta. My heart was racing. Rambo observed my movements without any sign of interest.

'Come on!' Thinking along the lines of 'all right then, be a good Rambo,' I tried to smile at the beast and slipped the safety catch off my gun. Our eyes took each other's measure. Just as I was about to pull the trigger, Rambo grabbed me. He did not bite, he grabbed. Like a wolf trap – just once. And held on, just like a wolf trap. My shot went wide of the mark. I lay on the ground, screaming, my arm between his jaws. The teeth had penetrated my sleeves and embedded themselves directly in my flesh. Granted, he did not bite my arm off. Calmly, without any particular effort, he stood above me. A dog who tore flesh the way other dogs dozed in the sun. Twigs were cracking behind me. Crazed with pain, I roared: 'Get your fucking dog off of me!' I tried to see the asshole who was his master, but Rambo didn't let me. Whoever that asshole was, I hated him, hated him even more than I hated his bull terrier. There was a draft of air, my skull exploded, and I zoomed into the void.

'Wake up, my friend. Wake up…'

A smooth warm hand stroked my forehead. I squinted.

At first I didn't see anything, and when my eyes focused, all I saw was concrete. Concrete ceiling, concrete walls, even my head seemed filled with concrete. Fluorescent lights glared from the walls around me. I remembered the generator. The room was approximately twenty by sixty feet. No windows and no sign of any heating or anything else. To the left and right, along the walls, sat some thirty people on rough wooden benches, giving me questioning looks. On the floor between the benches three children were playing with marbles. Now and again the marbles clicked and there was a brief whispered exchange. Otherwise all was quiet.

The hand touched me again. I forced my head to turn a little and looked into the wrinkled face of a black man who held me on his lap and quietly repeated his 'wake up'. His voice had the reassuring timbre of smokers who have managed to grow old. While I tried my best to comply with his wish, a woman in a glittering red outfit whispered something in Arabic, and a fat guy next to her nodded. It seemed to me they had decided I wouldn't be much help.

After what seemed a long time. I managed to sit up. Keeping my eyes closed, I managed to find a cigarette and put it in my mouth. The back of my head felt funny, and when I squeezed it, oozed red liquid. The black man gave me a light and smiled. He had to be at least seventy. His hair was short, grey, and wiry, and he wore a dark blue suit with a handkerchief in his breast pocket, shirt and tie, patent leather shoes, and a whiff of expensive perfume. Next to me in my muddy and bloody clothes – my right sleeve hung in shreds – he looked like one of the truly wealthy who find it amusing to mingle with the common folk sometimes and to enjoy a hot dog in their company. I smoked and examined the consequences of Rambo's repulsion of the Turkish invasion. Gingerly I picked bits of fabric out of the wound and tried to keep my arm elevated. Then I scanned the silent circle of faces. The place felt like a cross between a dentist's waiting room and an air-raid shelter.

I cleared my throat. 'Is there, by any chance, a lady here by the name of Sri Dao Rakdee?'

No one answered. Nothing changed in the expressions of three Thai women huddling in a corner. Before I had recovered from my surprise and disappointment, a fellow with two black brushstrokes under his nose and a lot of gold in his face asked me: 'Who are you?'

'Kemal Kayankaya, private investigator.'

Now all of them looked startled. The children stopped tossing marbles, and my Samaritan moved a little farther from me. From all sides came the choral exclamation: 'Police!?'

I shook my head very gently. 'No.'

Deep breaths. A pause, then the next question: 'Are you here for papers?'

That was the glitter lady.

'I'm looking for a Mr Larsson who claims he is able to provide people with forged identity papers.'

'What's that supposed to mean?'

'Aren't you here because you don't have residence permits?'

Some people looked tense again, others avoided my eyes.

All of them acted as if the question did not apply to them. I pointed at the door: 'Is it locked?'

A lean character out of a jeans ad, with lots of patches on his jacket and Walkman earphones round his neck, stood up and said: 'What if it is? It's for protection. So no one can find us – it's quite all right.' He repeated that for emphasis: 'Totally perfectly all right.'

'But what if no one at all comes to find you? And they just forget about you? I assume that Mr Larsson, or whatever his name is, has already received his fee?'

'He even got our jewellery,' the glittering lady lamented.

'All our jewellery!'

'Oh, that jewellery. He just took it because most of us didn't have enough money. He let me keep my Walkman.'

My adoptive father scratched his chin.

'That's just a piece of plastic.'

The jeans guy gave him a contemptuous look.

'Just like your patent leather pumps, Grandpa. Haven't seen a pair of those since we had to leave Iran ten years ago. You're totally retro, Gramps, totally retro – what do you want a German passport for? Go back to Oogah-Boogah and pick bananas.'

The old man smiled.

'We're all here for the same reason.'

'Sure…' The guy looked around. 'Only I'm not as scared as you are. This Larsson is on the level. I had a word with him yesterday, I told him that I am Ramin Ben Alam, so don't even dream about fucking us over. He heard me. Then we talked about movies, Eddie Murphy and so on.'

'You've been locked in here since yesterday?'

'Yesterday afternoon.'

'And before that, you were downstairs in the villa?'

He nodded.

'Did Larsson explain why you had to move?'

'Because of that neighbour. The old bag called the cops.'

I forgot my demolished skull and leaned forward. 'Really?'

'Right. I told you, we're here for our own protection.'

Suddenly it dawned on me why the immigration office had no file on Rakdee when I visited them. And that wasn't the only thing that dawned on me. But the question remained: what was going to happen now? I leaned back slowly and carefully.

'When will you receive your papers?'

'Tonight.' He beamed. 'Then we'll party. First a great dinner with my girlfriend, and then we'll disco down at the Marilyn.' He took a couple of dance steps, wiggled his hips and croaked, in English, 'I'm bad, I'm bad, I'm bad – yeah…'

People observed him with pity. He tossed his head back. 'Yeah, with my girlfriend Gabi, Gabi Schmittke!'

I extinguished my cigarette butt. 'This Larsson, did he have tattoos on his arms?'

The old man sitting next to me nodded.

'And what does the guy look like who brought me in?'

Two girls in headscarves giggled. A little fellow with a goatee got up and raised his arms to indicate something as wide as a wardrobe. 'Much meat, much beard, and much, much smell.'

I sighed. Then I looked around. 'I don't suppose he brought you anything to eat or drink?'

No response. The goateed fellow sat down again.

'And what if he won't bring you anything tonight, either? What if he won't be back, ever?'

People stared at the floor. I got up, swayed to the door and checked if it could be dealt with. One might as well have tried to kick the concrete wall in. When I turned back, the children were clinging to their voluminous mother. One of them was crying, her face smeared with bunker dust and tears. The other two watched me with wide-open eyes.

Suddenly I got furious. "'So no one can find you" – what a great idea! Larsson has collected his money, you haven't told anyone who you were going to meet, and the cops are glad that you're gone.' I spread out my hands and barked: 'We'll all die of suffocation here, most likely!'

Now the other two kids were crying, too, and a palpable atmosphere of fear spread in the room. Even the kid in jeans looked troubled. The dream of a life outside the hells of Beirut, Tehran, Colombo, or Istanbul seemed to vanish into thin air. The military, murdered relatives, torture, and hunger were suddenly present. Someone screamed. The old man closed his eyes.

They had fled. They had travelled halfway around the world with two suitcases. They had filled out applications, they had been rejected, they had applied again and had been rejected again, they had sought shelter in barns or shared a room with nine others. They had gone into hiding and lived without papers, and now they wanted to get at least these forged ones. Out of the void they had conjured up three thousand marks – they had tried everything just to be able to say, one day: tomorrow I'll sleep late, or I'll save up for a video recorder, I should be able to get one next year, or this weekend I'll get so smashed I'll crawl home, and if a cop shows up, I'll just stand up and pull out my wallet. But they never had a chance. Those who were rejected would remain so: the refugee 'in whose native culture torture is a common and traditional method of interrogation:' the refugee 'who, if he had not become politically active, need not have feared reprisals – and who was fully conscious of the risks of his activity;' and the 'economic asylum seeker' who is labelled a parasite in the world of German supermarkets, as if hunger and poverty were a kind of 'human right' for three quarters of the planet's population. He or she was merely the ghost of the 'at our expense' notion, never mind the fact that we have lived for centuries at his expense, and that he is trying to go where 'our' pedestrian malls, 'our' air force and 'our' opera houses have been built – at his expense. He is a 'parasite,' never mind that coffee, rubber heels, and metal ores do not grow in the forests of Bavaria. Sooner or later these people would be caught and put on the next plane out. But now they had been cheated out of even that fate. While I lit another smoke, most of the others tried to calm down the screaming guy. The kids' mother uttered an excited burst of Arabic. Then she started scolding me.

'Why are you putting such bad thoughts into our heads?' And, pointing at the weeping children: 'See what you've done!'

I opened my mouth and shut it again. In the meantime, they had made the man lie down on a bench. Staring up at the ceiling he talked, in a breathless, monotonous blend of English and Tamil, about his native village. As far as I could understand, that village no longer existed, and he had been forced to do something to his daughter. The daughter did no longer exist, either. He was the only survivor of his family.

I sat down next to the old man who had erected an invisible wall around himself. Arms crossed over his chest, his gaze fixed on his patent leather shoes, he whispered:

121

'You shouldn't have said that. This is a room full of very many people. There's no room for fear.' And, after a pause: 'You think we are stupid, but we have no choice in the matter.' Then he got up, walked across the circle of people who looked as if they were at their wits' end, reached the man from the village, and put his hand on the man's forehead.

I clenched my teeth. Was it my fault that we were cooped up in this room? And wouldn't I be a victim, too, when we ran out of air? They could all go fuck themselves, for all I cared. I closed my eyes, chain-smoked, and hoped that someone would come over and tell me to stop polluting the air, giving me an excuse to punch them in the nose. But no one came. Or at least, no one came the way I had imagined.

After my fourth cigarette I heard the first siren. Then the second, the third, finally a whole concert. They approached rapidly, emitted one final howl, and fell silent. Then there was engine noise; there were commands and voices through megaphones, barking dogs and footsteps. A key turned in the lock, the door opened. I tossed the butt and listened to a whole bag of pennies dropping in my head.

The first man to enter was less than five feet tall, thin as a board and just as stiff. His uniform fit him like a second skin. A neat oval of facial hair framed his mouth; otherwise he was clean-shaven and exuded one of those masculine fragrances that make the air taste like soap. Legs far apart, he stood in the doorframe, holding a pistol in his right, a radio transmitter in his left hand. When he spoke it sounded as if he was chewing on ice cubes. 'On your

feet, chop chop, get in line. Need to check your papers.'
Two men in uniform armed with submachine guns took
up positions to the right and the left of the door. I was
one of those who remained seated.

'Come on, I told you, chop chop!'

'Good afternoon. Rank and serial number, please, or I
won't comply.'

The submachine guns swivelled quickly to point at my
chest. The faces above them, adolescent and pimply,
looked as if they thought they had to save the world, at
the very least, and were pretty damn scared by the
prospect. Trigger fingers jerked nervously back and forth.

'And tell your kids to put their toys down. We don't
want them to pull the trigger by mistake.'

The commanding officer dissected me with his eyes.
Then he moved his chin in my direction, and his cohorts
rushed forward. In no time at all they pulled me off the
bench, made me stand between them, and patted me
down. I no longer had my Beretta, and my wallet was
gone, too. My ID was in the wallet. With short, abrupt
steps, the commanding officer came up and stopped right
in front of me. I could feel his breath on my face; it
smelled of peppermint. Old Spice and peppermint. It was
a knockout.

'Your ID.'

'Your serial number.'

'One one two eight one eight. Inspector Hagebrecht.
Your ID.'

'Someone stole it.'

'Under arrest.'

'Just a minute!' I resisted. I stopped when they were

about to break my arms. 'I'm a German citizen.'

A thin smile appeared on his face.

'A likely story. Take him away.'

'When your boss hears about this, he'll take your head off. Then you'll be just four feet – ouch! I bet you're supposed to take care of this business as discreetly as possible. Good luck with telling your boss that Kemal Kayankaya is one of your refugees! Better start practising…'

Minutes later I had been handcuffed and put on the bus, next to a guard, and watched through the barred windows how people were escorted out of the bunker, one by one. Some had to be punched to make them move, others were carried, many were weeping. The children came last. Separated from their mother, they were dragged into a car. They were screaming. Their marbles scattered onto the muddy ground and lay there, blinking. I turned to my guard.

'Who sent you here?'

Staring straight ahead, his chin rigid, his cap pulled down low over his forehead, he mumbled: 'Official secret.'

'Doesn't it seem strange to you that your strike force leader had a key to that bunker?'

'Not within the parameters of my task to find that strange.'

After Hagebrecht had latched the bunker door and given marching orders, the vehicle column took off. We drove along the road through the woods back to the Gellersheim football field. I saw my Opel and through its back window the party angel. She was still fast asleep. We drove through Gellersheim and on to the autobahn. The driver turned on the radio, and the officers nodded their heads to the rhythms of Bavarian brass band music. It was raining. At the Frankfurt intersection we turned off in the direction of the airport.

Chapter 12

'... and I was going to Mannheim today. Haven't missed a game this year, not one minute. Even in Dortmund, I was there to the very end. And what an end it was. They scored six goals against us-six! Just imagine... After that I was quite fed up, but then – well, I just felt I couldn't leave the guys in the lurch, just like that. So I kept on going, every Saturday, and now we've got the worst behind us. With Bein and Falkenmayer on board, we may even make it to the UEFA Cup next year, or we'll get the championship, and then we'll be back on the international scene, and then –' He stopped and looked at the iron bars. Behind them lay an empty landing with green walls and three yellow light fixtures. The shadows cast by the bars divided our cell into narrow segments. Again, no windows. A tap stuck out of one wall, and next to it there was a dirty white plastic toilet. Seventeen of us were sitting there on iron bedsteads, grey blankets wrapped around our shoulders. People smoked in silence. The women had been locked up in another cell down the hall. Once in a while one of them would call out, and one of the men would answer. It sounded like a conversation between people who were drowning. We had been there for four hours. A female officer had brought us some bread.

This was the deportees' holding tank at Frankfurt airport. The next flight to Beirut left in four hours. It was a little past three.

I huddled next to the young guy with the brushstrokes under his nose and contemplated the glowing end of my cigarette. His name was Abdullah, he came from South Lebanon, and in four hours he would be on his way back there. In front of us, on the floor, lay a fellow Turk murmuring prayers. Now and again he stopped, raised his head, and explained something to me in Turkish.

Abdullah cracked his knuckles.

'But maybe it's just the way things balance out. The team stays on top, and I go down, or the other way round.'

'So, if you shoot yourself in the head, then Eintracht wins the championship?'

His tongue made clicking sounds against his palate. 'Fate is our master.' And, after a glance into the hallway: 'No, there really is a law that makes things balance out. For instance – after I passed my college entrance exam, my girlfriend took off. Honest to God.'

I nodded and blew smoke rings. I kept thinking about ways to save these people from their flights. Attorneys, newspapers, church people – as long as I was not allowed to make a phone call because the immigration police believed that they had to put me on the evening flight to Istanbul, it was all pretty pointless.

One of my smoke rings floated right onto the praying fellow's nose. He looked up, waved his arms furiously, and started talking a mile a minute. Maybe he had asthma? I shrugged and smiled apologetically. When he didn't stop babbling – my smile was set in concrete by then – Abdullah got irritated and intervened.

'Please get it through your thick skull – he doesn't understand a word you're saying. He's a Turk, all right, but he doesn't speak Turkish.'

'Is that so? But why? Is he too stupid?' The guy's upper lip curled disdainfully. 'Or is he ashamed?'

His German was almost perfect, and I was annoyed with myself for having tried to communicate with him in a kind of sign language.

'I never learned it, that's all.'

'What is your father's name?'

'What does that have to do with it?'

'What's his name?'

'Tarik Kayankaya.'

He waved his hand as if to say, 'There you are.' Then he said: 'Well, what did I say, you're a Turk.'

'Amazing. You found that out, just like that?'

'You're denying your origin!'

'Why don't you just go on praying a little more? And I'll stop smoking.'

His index finger shot forward and stopped, trembling, in front of my nose. 'Tomorrow night you'll be back home, and then you won't be able to pretend you're German!'

Abdullah spat on the floor. 'Yeah, terrific. Then he'll sit in the joint there, and get punched in the mouth three times a day, but when he gets out after twenty years, he'll be able to order a cup of coffee in Istanbul in perfect Turkish.'

Abdullah flashed his gold teeth. The pious guy scrutinised him from top to toe, turned up his nose, and hissed: 'I won't be bought. I'd rather be in prison in Turkey than plead for asylum in Germany.'

He had hardly finished when there was some commotion behind us. A Kurd peeled off his blanket, cursing, and crossed two bedsteads to get to the patriot. He looked like a guy who took better care of his fists than of his chin.

'Man, you're talking shit. You're talking a bunch of unbelievable shit!'

The Turk replied in Turkish. He must have struck a wrong note: the next moment he was flying through the air, crashing against the wall, and sliding back down to the floor like a wet rag with a nosebleed. A murmur ran through the cell. The Kurd stood in our midst like a commander of armies. His gaze swept the assembly with a 'try me' expression. He had to be a body builder or decathlon athlete; in any case, he seemed to enjoy throwing people around, and if the people happened to be Turks, that was even more fun. He just stood there and waited, long enough for the prayer enthusiast to scrape himself off the floor and to reel over to the Kurd again. One might have thought that courageous, but it was undeniably unhealthy, and Abdullah muttered 'What a raving idiot!' The Kurd cracked his knuckles and rolled his shoulders, and everyone present realised individually that there would be no joy in intervention. Just as the Kurd got ready for another throw, a door swung open and five cops came marching down the hall. Three men, one woman, and a dog, to be exact. Things got really quiet. The Turk and the Kurd retired into a corner. The patrol of five stopped in front of our cell, and the woman took a piece of paper out of her breast pocket.

'Chatem, Abdullah.'

Abdullah's brown face turned a cheesy yellow, and I could no longer hear him breathe. The woman put her piece of paper away and unlocked the door. The men and the dog entered the cell. I motioned to Abdullah to remain seated and to keep his trap shut.

'Step forward.'

I got up.

'Come with us.'

'Where to?'

'Your flight leaves in an hour,' the woman explained. She was still standing in the hall. 'We told you the wrong flight this afternoon.'

Surrounded by the men and the dog, I left the cell. A murmur arose behind me, some of the men uttered quiet curses. Suddenly a voice called out: *'Allah yardimcin olsun!'* The door slammed shut, and someone else growled: 'He's on the side of the cops, your Allah.'

My last glimpse of the refugees was the old guy in patent leather shoes. He was loosening his tie.

She had the modest hair pulled back in a bun, the unornamented hands, the compassionate voice and the pale thin-lipped face of a nun, combined with the furtive eyes of a feminist in all-male company. On her, the freshly starched and ironed uniform was as becoming as a cardboard box. Her feet were clad in brown hiking boots, and between her breasts hung a necklace of light blue stones. She played with it whenever she was thinking things over. I sat there for ten minutes, arms crossed on my chest, two cops standing guard behind me, on a wooden chair and watched her search for Abdullah's passport in several metal cabinets, desk drawers, and file folders. Not a word had been said. On the wall facing me hung a calendar put out by the Border Guard. The picture showed one of its helicopters against a sunset.

I looked at the clock. If she had told the truth, Abdullah's plane was leaving in forty minutes. To prevent his being on it, I would have to sit here for another half-hour. And the passport had to remain misplaced. It would be even better if she could be distracted from the search. I took care of that.

'May I go to the men's room?'

'No.'

'I'm supposed to pee in my shoe?'

A washrag landed on my shoulder.

'Let's keep calm, colleague.'

'Did you hear that, sister? He called me colleague. That's defamation. Tell the guy –'

'Please, Mr Chatem…' Her tone reminded me of the kind of whole-wheat pedagogue who is able to smile a student into the ground and out of school. The voice was gentle and understanding, and she moved her arms as if she wanted to embrace me. Everything about her pretended to be soft and warm, but her eyes shone hard and cold as steel: '… if you could just be patient for a moment.'

131

Although it wasn't a question, she seemed to be waiting for a reply. I bowed my head: 'Sorry, Mrs Commissar, I'm a little nervous... What are my twenty-seven wives going to say after they haven't heard from me for such a long time? And my grandfathers, and my mother, oh Allah, my mother! She'll put me back in the sheep pen, the way she did when I let my brother Hassan play with that hand grenade –'

'Mr Chatem!'

She slapped the desk with her palm and looked stern. Then she strode past me and hunkered down in front of a cabinet. The ribbed contours of her underwear showed through the fabric of her trousers. I turned my head and drawled: 'She's got some hot little panties, doesn't she, your boss?'

Before one of the brothers could react, she turned, still sitting back on her heels. She hissed at me. 'What did you say?'

'I said I'm sure you're hot to trot, and why don't we have a little foursome? We've got a few minutes, don't we?'

Her stare lasered into my forehead. She got up slowly and walked toward me. Her left hand played with the necklace.

'What did you say I was?'

'I said you were hot to trot. To fuck. Fuck, or screw...' With a silly grin on my face, I turned to my guards and shouted: 'Screw, screw, screw!' Then back to her: 'And let me tell you, I'm hung. Back home, the folks call me Ali the Flagpole.'

Her pupils had contracted. I winked at her: 'And when

I say beam, sweetie, I mean *pole.*'

She slapped me so fast and so hard that I fell off my chair. While I was still on the floor, the door opened. I raised my head and froze. The tall grey-haired man with the angular face stopped in the doorway and took in the scene. His voice sounded a little hoarse when he asked: 'What is going on here?'

'Mr Chatem has insulted me.'

'Chatem?'

I grabbed the edge of the desk, pulled myself up, brushed off my sleeves. 'The sister is referring to me.'

Höttges closed the door, thrust his hands into his pockets, and walked slowly up to me. Once again his cold grey eyes held mine. Without turning away, he said: 'Mrs Henkel, leave the room, please.'

'But, Commissioner, what does that –'

'And take the officers with you.'

By the door, she turned back. 'Should I make a reservation for him on the next flight?'

'Just leave!'

After the three had left us alone in the office, I leaned against the edge of the desk and lit a cigarette. Höttges followed my actions with his eyes. Otherwise he was motionless.

'So, what do you know, I did hit the right office yesterday morning, didn't I? Do you know the reason that Larsson, or Manne, or whatever his name was, gave for transporting the refugees from the villa to the bunker? He claimed that a neighbour had called the police. The same neighbour Klaase wasn't allowed to tell me about in your office – because you knew it was a hot tip. Even if the rationale for the move was an invention – because the real reason for it was – Larsson could have found out about the neighbour *only from you!'*

He had remained stone-faced, but the skin around his nose had paled visibly. Now he looked down, and the muscles around his jaw twitched. I couldn't tell whether he was about to fold or whether he would try to shut me up. I knocked the ash off my cigarette.

'And that explains why the gang was so well informed about people who had been issued deportation orders. They had it from the horse's mouth – from you, the man who issues those orders. Inspector Hagebrecht's key to the bunker was the final clue. I'm sure he is not in on the scheme, but he's not the kind of guy who would wonder where his superior officer had obtained such a key. What I can't understand is why your partners didn't let you know about me? It was really stupid to lock me up in the bunker.'

He was still staring at the floor. Then he turned his back to me and started pacing. 'You're in no position to harm me,' he said. His voice was firm but strained.

'That's correct. A few refugees hide in a bunker, are discovered by the police, get deported. They are illegal aliens, and from a purely legal point of view, they get what they deserve.' I dropped the butt, stepped on it, lit another one. 'Or that would be all there was to it – if I hadn't found a corpse in Gellersheim.'

He stopped. 'A corpse?' Then, haltingly, he resumed his pacing. His face reflected a blend of fright and the confirmation of his worst fears. I nodded. 'And even though it's unlikely that you committed that murder, and even though nothing else can be traced back to you, I can still get you some publicity that won't smell too sweet. It might even lead to things like suspension, dismissal, loss of pension.'

He had stopped by the window and was looking at the police parking lot and the entrance to the arrival hall. A family returning from vacation in colourful hats, sandals, and socks made their way through the sliding doors. The son was wearing a pair of diving goggles.

Höttges cleared his throat. 'How much?'

'Not how much. I want the file.'

'What file?'

'The one you made disappear yesterday morning. The Rakdee file.'

A pause. He looked out the window again. 'Is that all?'

'No. Give orders to the effect that none of those people will be deported for the time being; that they get a chance to speak to their attorneys; and that they get some real food brought to their cells.'

He nodded. His expression almost made me feel sorry for him. I gave him a sceptical look. 'No need to be so down in the mouth. Until now you've always acted the sergeant major. It's your job to hunt people. But to rob them of their money and jewellery, in cahoots with mobsters – if someone happens to tread on your toes after that, you might as well hang on to the old stiff upper lip.'

When he raised his head again, he had aged years. His eyes were murky, and the angular chin was just a brittle and trembling bone. Then he shouted: 'What do you know about it! In cahoots with mobsters! Once in my life, I made a mistake!'

I put out my cigarette. 'Should I hazard a guess? Köberle found out about that mistake, and you've been on his list of collaborators ever since.'

I pushed off from the desk, went to the door, and put my hand on the doorknob. By the window stood a broken man staring at an empty parking lot.

'Anybody can get involved with crooks, and then get blackmailed by them. But as an immigration officer I find you simply disgusting. That file will be in my mailbox by tomorrow morning. And don't even think about warning Köberle. If he calls, just tell him I'm on my way to Istanbul. Good day.'

Chapter 13

Ten minutes later I stood in the phone booth by the Pan Am desk and called every newspaper and organisation I could think of to tell them about the pending mass deportation. The last call I made was to Benjamin Weiss, director of an advice centre for refugees, occasional bass player with the legendary club combo The Wicherts from Next Door, and decent skat player. We knew each other from our university days. He had started out majoring in philosophy, I in law, and we had both dropped out after a year. He, because he began to suffer from insomnia and thought this was caused by his ability to master half the material during lectures; I, because I couldn't stand the surrounding adolescents constantly snapping their legal briefcases open and shut. Now Weiss lived with his wife, two sons, and fifty shelf feet of jazz records in Gallus, and when he wasn't working, he was either sick or flying kites with the kids. At the office, there was no reply, and it was too dark to be flying kites. At his home number the phone rang four times until a weak voice replied. 'Ye-es?'

'Kayankaya here. There's thirty people at the airport about to be deported.'

'How many?'

'Thirty.'

'If this is supposed to be an April Fool's joke – I'm in bed with strep throat.'

'No joke. They had *me* locked up there with those people – I just got out a moment ago.'

Somehow, he managed to emit an amused noise from his afflicted larynx. 'So where did they want to send you?'

'I suggested Sardinia.'

He repeated that noise, then asked: 'What exactly happened?'

'It's a long story. Why don't you come over?'

'OK. I'll be there in half an hour.'

'I'll be in the departure hall.'

We hung up. I jingled my change for a minute before I put it in the slot and dialled Weidenbusch's number. After I had given him a broad outline of the progress of my investigation, all the way to the bunker, I paused briefly, then said: 'But, sad to say, your girlfriend wasn't there.'

'No? Are you sure?'

'Pretty damn sure. Unless she didn't want to be recognised.'

'But even so I would think she'd have contacted me in the meantime.'

'She may be unable to do that.'

'What do you mean? If she wasn't in the bunker –'

'Maybe someone has other plans for her.'

He gulped audibly and asked me to excuse him for a

moment. I heard him open a bottle, pour a drink, and smack his lips; then he came back to the phone and sounded full of resolve: 'She must have been scared. That's why she didn't say anything. I'm sure she's in that holding cell! I'll go to the airport.'

'How come you're so excited, all of a sudden? Yesterday you told me you wanted to get rid of her.'

'Oh, that was just a bunch of bullshit. I was totally exhausted. Please forget what I told you yesterday.'

Weidenbusch came waddling through the waiting area, holding on to his belly with both hands, as I was enjoying coffee and ham on toast and perusing a travel brochure. Panting, he sat down and yelped: 'Where are the cells?' The West End yuppie accustomed to sipping red wine had turned into a derelict barfly. He reeked of alcohol and cigarettes, his hair hung into his face, his shirt front was stained, and his eyes had dark rings around them and gleamed feverishly. He took off his glasses and wiped the sweat off his forehead.

I waved my thumb. 'Down the moving walkway, turn right, go outside, cross the parking lot. If they don't let you in, ask for Commissioner Höttges and mention my name.'

'But – you're not coming with me?'

I shook my head. 'Your girlfriend isn't there. She is somewhere else.'

'How can you know that?'

'I can't. I just do.'

'Does that mean you'll go on looking for her?'

'Are you about to offer me another cheque?'

'No! Just because…' He ran the tip of his tongue across

his upper lip. Suddenly his demeanour changed. He got agitated: 'You treat me as if I were one of your suspects!'

Then, furious: 'But it was I who hired you, and if I feel like it, I can fire you, too!'

'Any time. Would you like to settle our accounts right now?'

Undecided, he fussed with his eyeglasses. Then he jammed them back on. 'I'm going to the cells. You'll receive your cheque, as agreed, and since we probably won't meet again –'

He hesitated. Should he shake hands or just leave with a nod?

I waved a piece of toast at him. 'If someone is exerting some kind of pressure on you because of Mrs Rakdee – I mean, someone apart from your mother – you better tell me about it.'

He looked completely bewildered. 'Don't you understand? You're fired!'

With that, he turned and disappeared into the grey-green mass of a group of senior tourists. I sat there and finished my toast. Soon after that the first journalists arrived. Loaded down with cameras, they trotted through the hall like a bunch of scared chickens, generating excitement among both travellers and personnel. A bomb, hijackers, the Prince of Monaco, or the Kessler Twins? Hundreds of pairs of eyes scanned doors, counters, and seats. Then I spotted Benjamin Weiss. His six-and-a-half-foot tall figure was clearly visible among a group in colourful outfits who stormed through the sliding doors carrying stacks of paper under their arms and immediately started leafleting everybody. I waved and

Weiss shuffled over. He was bundled up in an overcoat, scarf, and knitted cap, and what was visible of his face seemed to cry out for bed rest and hot lemon juice. He sank into a chair next to me, stretched his legs, and muttered: 'May I have a cigarette?'

'Not the best thing, in your condition – ?'

He repeated his request, emphatically.

I lit one and handed it to him. He took a deep drag and exhaled the smoke slowly.

'First one in three days. In bed, it's not so bad, but…' He took a second drag. 'I've been over there. They're holding exactly thirty-three of them. Three attorneys are talking with them now. The Protestant honcho has promised to help; the Catholic one is at a Silesian Displaced Persons dinner with Wallmann. The entire Social Democrat party is recording a disc for their election campaign, and the refugee ombudsman of the Greens is having a baby. Her replacement doesn't have a car but is trying to get here soon. What else – oh yes, the Multicultural Office: there, the cleaning woman answers the phone – she doesn't have a whole lot of German, but as far as I could make out, her employers are attending the opening of a castanet exhibit…' He stopped and sucked on his cigarette.

'You found all that out in half an hour?'

'Most of it. The rest I had no trouble making up. Now it's your turn.'

While Weiss kept sliding deeper into his chair, and his cap slowly descended over his eyebrows, I gave a brief description of the alleged forgery gang's M.O., without mentioning names or localities, and wound up by telling him: 'There's nothing that can be done legally, but I'll try to get their money and jewellery back.'

Glassy-eyed, Weiss stared into space for a while. Then he sighed and straightened up. 'Let's see what the attorneys can do about it. I'm going back to talk to them. Will I see you again today?'

'When I've found their money.'

'I'll probably stay here overnight.' He wrapped the scarf tighter around his neck. 'In case I don't see you again –'

'– I'll come by every day and smuggle a pack of smokes into your bed.'

'Do that. So,' he raised his arm feebly, 'good luck.'

'The same to you.'

He left, and I walked to the exit. A damp gust of wind met me at the door. I turned up my collar and hailed a cab with my good arm. 'To the nearest hospital.'

'Where's Heinz?'

'Dunno.'

I helped myself to a small open-face cheese sandwich.

'Is Slibulsky here?'

'Don't know that either.'

'Charlie?'

'I'm not allowed to know.'

I took a bite, chewed, studied her. She was in her early forties, built like a sumo wrestler. She wore a wig and a pale blue dress with a flower pattern and busied herself knitting a vest for a dog. On the table next to her lay Kohl in fifty pieces.

'So you're Heinz's wife?'

The knitting needles stopped clicking, and two hooded

eyes gave me the once-over.

'If what you mean by that is that I get to push him down the Zeile once a week in his wheelchair – yes, I am. And I get him his videos, and on Mondays I get him his football weekly. But I don't have to darn his socks. So, I can't complain.'

She pursed her lips in a hint of a smile. I smiled back, tossed two coins on the counter, and walked down the pink hallway past rows of female legs on both sides. Shoo-be-doo music trickled from speakers in the ceiling. It was almost eight-thirty in the evening. I joined the line of johns winding its way past the rooms and up the stairs all the way to the fourth floor and back. Up on the fourth, I stepped over a barrier that said 'Private', ascended two more landings and knocked on a rust-brown metal door. The door opened and Charlie peered out, a question mark on his face. He was wearing a white silk suit, no shirt, no shoes, and held a box of matchbox automobile models in one hand. When he recognised me, his mouth opened in amazement. Then he raised his arm in a welcoming gesture.

'Hey, what do you know, it's the little brown guy with the big mouth! Well, this is a surprise.' He shouted over his shoulder: 'Sweetheart? We've got company. Two glasses, and a bottle of Asbach!' Then, back to me: 'Let's have a drink!'

Without waiting for an answer, he grabbed my shoulder, kicked the door shut with his bare heel, and dragged me over to the couch. All over the glass table and the fluffy rug was an array of what looked like almost a thousand colourful little metal cars. On the table stood a bottle of rubbing alcohol next to a pile of white rags and a beaker filled with toothbrushes. While he kept kneading my shoulder with one hand, he picked up one of the cars with the other, held it up to the light, and exclaimed happily: 'Nineteen seventy-one, yellow jeep, brown top, tow bar – isn't it terrific?'

'Super-terrific.'

Carefully, he put the miniature back. 'My collection. Eight hundred and ninety-two models. I clean 'em up every spring, it's a job – but, snooper,' his hand waved across the colourful pile, 'tell me, ever see anything like it?'

'I need to have a word with you, Charlie.'

That startled him.

'I'm showing you my car collection, and you "need to have a word"?'

'You got it.'

His arm slid off my shoulder like a dead man's. Then he flashed a grin. 'I know what you need, snooper, you need a drink.' He patted my knee and snapped his fingers in the direction of the bathroom. 'Sweetheart – what's with those drinks?'

'Coming right up, Charlie.'

A girl entered the room. In her jeans, knit top, and gym shoes she looked no older than sixteen. She had a blue bow in her hair. She smiled politely at me and disappeared behind the bar. With her round snub-nosed face, small firm breasts, and an ass like two honeydew melons, she looked like a teenager who spends her mornings in the schoolyard, her afternoons at an ice cream parlour, and her evenings with the captain of the football team. That impression was marred, however, by a big green bruise around her right eye and bright red scratch marks on her cheeks and neck. She had tried to cover all that up with make-up, but the result made her look like a monster.

Charlie leaned back and gave me a wink. 'Sweet, eh?'

'A little worse for wear.'

He wagged his head. 'That'll pass.' And, louder: 'Right, sweetheart? In two or three days, I'll have my princess back.'

'Yes, Charlie.'

'You know I didn't mean any harm. On the contrary. It was just because I love you, and because I'm a proud man.'

'Yes, Charlie.'

'I don't think you'd have found a guy like me in Klein-Mörlenbach. Right, sweetheart?'

'Absolutely right.'

After two snifters of Asbach had been set down next to the matchbox cars, and the girl had retired to the bed with a notepad and a pencil, we clinked glasses to eternal friendship. Then I asked him: 'Do you know a guy who looks like a steam roller and answers to the name Axel?'

'Sure do. Big Beef Axel. Was a pretty good heavyweight once. Now he deals in used cars and motorbikes.'

'Including Toyotas?'

'He drives one. Why?'

'Is it a silver-coloured jeep?'

He raised his eyebrows suspiciously. 'Are you trying to give me the third degree again?'

'I just want to know if this Axel drives a silver Toyota jeep.'

'What if he does? Is it against the law?'

'Does the name Höttges mean anything to you?'

'Never heard of it.'

'Commissioner Höttges of the immigration police.'

'Hey, man, am I a Negro? Why should I know any immigration cops?'

'But when I mentioned the name Köberle to him, he didn't seem particularly surprised.'

'He didn't, eh… Listen,' he gave me the stare, 'what's all this bullshit?'

'Yesterday, I came to see you about Mrs Rakdee. Remember?'

He groaned. 'Oh, not that again.' He reached for the Asbach and leaned back. His toes toyed idly with the fluffy rug. 'So? Did you find her?'

'No. But I know who kidnapped her.'

'Yeah?' He swirled the brandy in the snifter.

'Yeah. A guy named Manne. But he's just one of a gang. The others are Höttges, Axel, Slibulsky, and…'

I watched him out of the corner of my eye. His surprise seemed genuine. His voice grew deep and ominous.

'What are you telling me, snooper?'

'They tell refugees, illegal aliens, that they can provide them with forged papers. The refugees pay three thousand marks a head, and then they get locked up in a predetermined location where Höttges and his guys come and pick them up. Today they got thirty of them; that's a total of ninety thousand marks. It's really a smart and simple scam… And I think your brother is the one who came up with it.'

'Heinz did?'

He grabbed my lapels and came so close that I felt his breath. 'Say that again.'

'Get your hands off me first.'

'I'll keep them on you as long as I please. So?'

'A man by the name of Köberle is involved in this business. And if it isn't you –'

'Is there any evidence for that?'

'No, but it fits, and it's enough for the news hounds.'

'The papers…?'

He gave me a searching look, and his grip on me relaxed.

Then he shook himself and hissed: 'Man, if you're shitting me, I'll turn you into hamburger. But if it is true,' he let go of me, 'my brother's sold his last chocolate bar.'

After another searching glance, he rushed to his closet and tossed shoes, socks, and a shiny grey suit into the room. The girl had almost stopped breathing. Hiding behind her notepad under the covers, she watched Charlie's actions and seemed to consider if it would be wiser to pick up his things or to play dead. Suddenly he stopped and leaned against the closet door, his jaw jutting out at an angle.

'Why are you telling me all that stuff?'

'First of all because I want to know where the gang is hanging out now.'

'I have no idea.'

'And secondly, as I told you, I don't have any proof, and since the cops are involved in it, an official investigation would be over before it even began. Charlie, I want you to kick some ass.'

His shoulders stretched the fabric of his white jacket. 'Don't worry, I will. But, you know,' he shuffled his feet on the rug, 'it would be best not to go to the papers right away. I want to take care of this before my boss finds out about it. Otherwise it might look as if I had no control over my boys here.'

I nodded. 'Eberhard Schmitz wouldn't like that.'

Charlie looked at me. 'No, he wouldn't like it at all.' There was a curiously ecstatic expression in his eyes.

'All right then. I'll wait until tomorrow night.'

His eyes cleared. A grateful smile.

'You're OK, snooper.'

While he changed, picked a shirt and checked his tie in front of a mirror, he kept up a steady stream of curses. I twirled a cigarette between my fingers and waited. 'My brother's in cahoots with the cops – God, I'm glad our Mum's no longer alive. She was the greatest whore in all of Sachsenhausen – what a body... She was the toast of the whole fucking Occupation Zone. "Boys," she used to say, "boys, remember one thing: never tell the cops anything. Only a cowardly swine would call the cops. It was cops who dragged your grandpa to the ovens."'

He shook his head. 'And now the fucking crip goes and helps them rip off bimbos...'

He slewed around to glance at the bed. All that could be seen was a hank of hair.

'Hey, you silly little cunt, pay attention when I'm talking about my family!'

Slowly, her face emerged. 'But Charlie, I'm listening.'

He growled contemptuously, over his shoulder. 'That's what she always says. But all she really wants to do is write letters to her girlfriends, "Frankfurt is so exciting" and "oh, I'm so happy here..."' He jabbed the air in front of her face with his index finger. 'What would your friends say if they saw you looking like that? Eh?'

And, while he took a .32 automatic out of a drawer in the bedside table: 'And anyhow, what's the use writing letters when you can pick up the phone?'

The girl had pulled the covers over her head. The bedspread trembled like a sick dog. Charlie slapped the clip into the gun. 'Don't think I give a shit about your bawling.'

I checked my watch. It was nine-fifteen.

'Charlie?'

'Yeah?'

'Where you headed with that cannon?'

'Where...' He stuck the automatic in his waistband.

'... Oh, have a beer, get a little fresh air...'

'That suits me just fine. I could use a beer.'

'Oh yeah?'

I got up and went to the window. It was raining again. The wind was blowing the rain almost horizontally down the street, and the wet windowpane made the neon signs look like runny watercolours. People huddled in entrance ways.

'A little fresh air never hurt anyone.'

Charlie scratched his ass pensively.

'Just take care you don't catch a cold.'

Chapter 14

The cloud cover tore open and moonlight flooded the premises of Wolf's Car Repair Shop. To the right, a pile of hubcaps, to the left, a heap of rusty fenders, and behind that, car doors of every shape and size. A narrow puddled road led past the mounds of scrap to a flat building at least fifty metres long. Half of the building was occupied by the shop. The other half was taken up by an office and a storeroom for parts. Cars were parked in front of it, among them the silver Toyota jeep. A wide-mesh wire fence ran around the perimeter, with a locked entry gate and two rough-hewn wooden doors, both of them unlocked. We slipped in through one of them and cautiously walked up to a wide concrete slab in front of the office door. It stood ajar. A narrow beam of light fell on our mud-encrusted shoes.

Charlie pulled his automatic. 'You go first.'

I shook my head. 'Guy with the artillery goes first.'

He prodded my chest with the gun. 'You first.'

I said, 'As you wish,' and put my hand on the doorknob. It didn't look like an easy trick to slip on the concrete step, but I was going to try my best. I jerked the door open to the left, shifted my weight to the right, and spun around like a top. The edge of my hand struck Charlie straight in the stomach. While he bent over, gasping for air, I punched him twice in the face. His nose cracked and blood ran over his mouth. With an incredulous expression on his face, he crashed down on the gravel. I picked up his automatic, rubbed my knuckles, and listened. Except for Charlie's subdued groans, the place was as quiet as a graveyard.

I prodded him with the tip of my shoe and hissed, 'Get up.'

He was holding his remodelled face with one hand, clutching gravel with the other. He managed to raise his head and stare at me.

'What was that –'

'Shut up, and get up.' I pointed the automatic at his forehead. 'One –'

By the time I said two, he was on his feet.

'Onward.'

Like a drunken sailor he staggered to the door, leaned against it and stumbled into the entrance hall, a rough corridor with a bare light bulb and rusty coat hooks on the wall. Two grey blankets hung over the entrance to the storeroom. Behind them, a radio was playing. I grabbed Charlie's collar and stuck the automatic in his ear. 'Not a peep.'

He trembled. We approached the entrance slowly. Now we could hear voices over the radio music. When we got to the blankets, I gave Charlie a shove that made him fly inside, head first, I jumped after him and crashed into a shelf full of headlights. Axel and Slibulsky were sitting at a table with two bottles of beer and a pile of jewellery in front of them. They looked thunderstruck. Then Axel pulled a .221 Remington Fire Ball, a weapon suitable for hunting elephants or shooting down small aircraft; one could also use it as a weight to hold down the roof in a hurricane –but for fast shooting, it's about as useful as an eggbeater.

My first bullet struck his shoulder, the second his forearm. As he slid off his chair, roaring, I crawled over the stack of headlights, grabbed his black monster gun, and jumped to one side, both my guns at the ready.

'Next guy makes a move I don't like, I'll drill a hole in his skull!'

No one was even contemplating such a move. No one, that is, who knew what a gun is. I heard his paws hit the floor, then a throaty sound and panting. I whipped around and fired twice without looking. It was incredible. Even though the Remington had torn off half of his side, Rambo kept coming. Dragging his bloodstained ass across the floor, showing no sign of pain, he charged me on three legs. I pulled the trigger again, and I had to pull it four more times before the animal, deformed into a red blob, finally lay there motionless. I took a deep breath. Then I turned. Charlie lay whimpering between two oil cans, Axel had curled up in pain under the table, and Slibulsky looked paralytic. He surveyed the battlefield with an absentminded stare, seemingly trying to figure out what was going on. When that stare got around to me, it skipped.

'Slibulsky.'

'Mm-hmm…?'

I got up and went to the table.

'You have a gun?'

He raised his left arm slowly, raised his right arm, still in its plaster cast, and shook his head. Our eyes met for a moment. His were empty, expressionless as buttons. I indicated that he could put his hands down again.

'Turn off the radio and take care of Fatso.' I turned. 'Charlie! Join the company.'

While Slibulsky heaved Axel onto the chair and Charlie came stumbling over, holding a handkerchief to his mouth, I looked around the room. Tall metal shelves filled with spark plugs, fan belts, and other parts stood in tight rows stretching to the end of the room. No windows, no ventilation. Dirty yellow light was provided by a row of caged light bulbs strung diagonally across the ceiling.

'Any more of those monsters here?'

No response. Chin on chest, holding his shoulder, Axel leaned over the table and breathed heavily. Now and again he opened his mouth, but all that came out was saliva. I stuck his Remington behind my belt.

'All right. You first, Charlie.'

He removed the handkerchief, let the hand holding it rest on his lap. Still pretending innocence, he said: 'Me? But why me?'

I'd had enough condescension from a pimp. Before Charlie could raise his arms, I slapped him, hard enough for the sound to echo across the room. He covered his face with his hands.

'Shut up and listen to what I have to say.' I lit a cigarette and started pacing. I was furious. 'Since you like to think that everybody else is an idiot, you had to check me out yesterday morning, in person. Slibulsky could have taken care of that quite unobtrusively, and I wouldn't have suspected from the very beginning that you either knew who kidnapped Mrs Rakdee or were involved in it yourself. In the meantime, I had some other ideas, but when Slibulsky panicked and tried to send me on a wild goose chase – if not before – I decided to pay attention to you again. And, of course, to Slibulsky.'

I took a drag on my cigarette. Slibulsky didn't move. He had been motionless for the last five minutes, resting his good arm on the cast and staring holes into the floor.

'The anonymous note was a gigantic mistake. Not only because of the shaky handwriting – it looked exactly like something written by a right-handed person who has to use his left – but also because I was bound to realise, at the After Hours if not before, that the note was meant to distract me – from Gellersheim, since I hadn't planned on going anywhere else. And only *you* knew about that... So, while I was in the shower...' I had walked up to him. Now I reached into the inside breast pocket of his jacket and pulled out his Interconti notepad. Slibulsky reacted only by calmly smoothing the front of his jacket. I tossed the pad on the table.

'Then I did drive to Gellersheim, and so forth.'

I ground out the cigarette butt with my heel and kicked it under a shelf. Then I turned back to Charlie.

'At some point, Eberhard Schmitz told you about my visit, and you gave Axel orders to go to the villa. To take me to the bunker was the second big mistake. If Axel had just locked me up somewhere else for a day, the refugees could have been deported in all directions of the compass, and everything would have been hunky dory. Axel may be a big guy, but he's not all that smart. And that gets us back to you. As soon as I showed up at your place tonight, you realised that I had to be eliminated. Schmitz had given you the use of the villa, and if anything happened there, you were responsible. So you decided to pretend that it was all your brother's doing, a pretty dumb idea, especially considering that it was I who suggested it. I don't know what your plan was – maybe you were going to tell these two to liquidate me by tomorrow morning. All I know is that if I had come through this door first, I wouldn't have stood much of a chance of informing the press.'

The only sound in the room came from the humming lights. Slibulsky was chewing on a matchstick, Axel had closed his eyes, Charlie was patting his nose with the handkerchief. They looked like three guys who had gone in on a Porsche and then totalled it immediately. While the wrecker was picking up the pieces, everyone realised how much he disliked the other two.

I lit a new one and took a couple of drags. 'Now as for you, Slibulsky – I had been hoping all along that I was mistaken. I didn't think you were the kind of guy who robs every last dime from people and then sends them off to their deaths. You're working for Charlie, so if he tells you to keep an eye on me – that's all right. And since you couldn't just go back to him and tell him that I was on my way to Gellersheim, you had to write that note. But now I see you here, divvying up the spoils, and that goes beyond your duties as an employee. What's your share?

Twenty, thirty thousand? And a kilo of earrings? You're just another one of those cheapskates who will crawl into any sewer if there's money in it.'

Slibulsky kept chewing his match and staring holes into the floor. Only his left hand had now moved into his pocket for warmth.

Charlie cleared his throat, discreetly.

'I hope you realise that you're just making up a bunch of shit.'

I went to the table, picked up a handful of jewellery and flung it into his face.

'And what about that? Is that just a bunch of shit?'

He started jabbing his index finger into the air and screeched hysterically: 'You're out of your mind, snooper, you're completely out of your mind!' Then, to Slibulsky: 'Tell your buddy that he's out of his mind – tell him to take the money and leave us alone!'

'Are you guys crazy?' Axel emerged from his stupor. His face, as far as it was visible in all that hair, was pale and contorted by hate. Beads of sweat were dripping off his eyelashes. 'You're scared of this asshole – *this* asshole?'

He turned, spraying a trail of blood on the floor.

'What do you think would happen if I told the cops that you wanted to liberate that bunch of illegals – eh? Those guys don't give a shit about noble ideals, any more than we give a shit about your talk about friends! Listen, Ali, we're not in the Balkans here – and Slibulsky is no Sir Galahad! None of us gives a shit if your dago brothers are sent home!'

'They're not being sent home. They –'

'I know, they get offed. Let me tell you, Ali, I wipe my

ass with your bleeding heart!'

There was a pounding in my temples. I pulled the Remington out, slowly, and aimed the revolver at his left eye, the automatic at the right. 'Where is the money?'

The holes in his arm must have deprived him of all common sense. His eyes open wide, he hissed: 'You wouldn't dare,' and his shadow advanced toward me. 'We've been putting up with your shit long enough. Check your knees, they're shaking. You're just a bad April Fool's joke. So why don't you just say "April Fool," and give my gun back, and fuck off!'

He was only inches away from grabbing the guns. Blood began to boil in my ears. Suddenly, a voice behind me said 'April Fool!' There were two gunshots, and Axel's head snapped back, now covered in a paste of brains and hair. He was dead before the echoes of those shots subsided.

Charlie shook. He had jumped up from his chair and was staring at the huge bleeding body toppling to the floor. He turned as pale as only a man shaking with fear in a dirty yellow light could turn pale. A red puddle was spreading out around Axel's head. I turned. Slibulsky sat where he had been sitting all along. The only difference was that he held a pistol in his left hand. Slowly he slipped it back into the side pocket of his jacket and took the match out of his mouth. His lips twitched a little.

Without a word we dragged the corpse past fenders and hubcaps to a grassy spot where the ground was softer. While Charlie kept vomiting between two wrecked cars, Slibulsky and I dug a hole. The moon stood directly overhead. I seemed to be evolving into a gravedigger.

After the ground had been flattened out again and the shovels had been returned to their shed, Slibulsky handed me my wallet. I went to the office to order two taxicabs. Meanwhile, Slibulsky got a black suitcase from the Toyota. After that we went back to the warehouse, stuffed the dead dog into a plastic bag, and collected the jewellery.

The three of us regained the street, and I dropped the plastic bag into a public wastebasket. Green-faced, Charlie leaned against a lamppost, staring vacantly into space and crumbling a small cigar between his fingers. Slibulsky sat on the curb. I stepped into the light of the streetlamp and lit a cigarette.

'If any of this becomes public, I'll blame it all on you – a fight over the loot, something like that. If that should happen, Schmitz's name would hit the papers, too, and I'm not sure who would get the worst of his fury, you or me.'

Charlie nodded.

A little later, the first cab arrived, and Charlie got in. Soon after that the second one came, and Slibulsky and I got in the back with our suitcase full of money and the bag of jewellery. I told the cabbie to take us to the airport.

We rode in silence for a while, and the cabbie cast several suspicious glances at us in the rearview mirror. Then he started to discuss the pointlessness of Daylight Saving Time, all by himself, and all by himself he stopped discussing it. Finally he decided to turn on the radio.

When we got to the autobahn, I asked Slibulsky: 'Why didn't you hand me that gun?'

Leaning forward a little, Slibulsky fussed with his cast.

'You already had two,' he replied without looking up. 'No one can use three guns at the same time.'

'But if I had really searched you, how do you think I would have reacted?'

Slibulsky didn't say anything. I looked out the window at the passing lights of American high-rises. My arm throbbed, and I could still feel the tetanus and rabies shots in my ass.

'What I don't understand is why Schmitz let you use that villa. Never mind what his cut may have been, those are ridiculous sums by his standards.'

'He gave it to us because Axel was his nephew.'

I gave a start. 'So it was Schmitz's nephew you –' I stopped myself just in time. The cabbie seemed to find it hard to get comfortable in his driver's seat. Slibulsky must have forgotten him, or he just didn't give a damn at that moment; in any case, he shrugged and said: 'Axel would have killed you. He kept ranting all day about his moment of weakness there in front of the bunker. And after his doggie got atomised... I had no choice. Unless you had pulled the trigger – and it didn't look like you would.'

When we arrived at the airport and I handed the driver his money, he did not look at me, and his hand shook.

On the way to the police sub-station I bought two football magazines. Then we had to wait a while until Benjamin Weiss got rid of a female reporter who had managed to get into the attorneys' room. She explained that she was working for the illustrated magazine Schampus and wanted to secure an exclusive 'picture story' on the refugees in the bunker. As they were released, the refugees could recreate scenes of that 'heavy time', and the 'kicker' would be that they would all be wearing 'the new Gaultier winter collection, with sunglasses, the women with veils but otherwise real sexy.'

After she was gone, we handed the money and the jewellery to Weiss. He drank a schnapps with us, chased it with aspirin, chain-smoked and told us that no one had been deported so far and that the attorneys thought no one would be during the next few days or weeks. Then I went to the cells and gave Abdullah the football magazines. We left the building. Outside, police guards with helmets and pistols were stationed at five-yard intervals. Facing them, a dozen reporters hung out next to a potted palm, passing thermos bottles to each other. The area between them was covered in discarded leaflets.

'Now what? Would you like me to buy you a drink?'

Slibulsky shook his head. 'I have a date with Schlumpi.'

'A midnight date?'

The sliding doors flew apart, and we entered the arrival hall. Slibulsky stopped. Looking determined, he told me: 'I think we're quits now, and if I have a midnight date with Schlumpi, then that is where I have to go. But we can have a drink afterwards.'

'If you're still able to lift a glass.'

He gave me a suspicious look. Then he waved his hand at the ceiling. 'I don't care what you think, but you better stay out of it.'

Chapter 15

The blocks around the railway station were really jumping. It was the Americans' night off, and the Eintracht team had taken a bath in Mannheim, zero to one. Frustrated GIs and even more frustrated football fans reeled down the pavements, and cars shaking with music were gridlocked around the block. Shell game artists gathered crowds on street corners. Flickering neon; honking horns, shouting and singing blended into one garish surge. We passed two derelicts fighting over a can of beer while a third one was busy spilling its contents over his shirt front and reached the entrance to The Smiling Die.

Slibulsky went inside. I sat down on the trunk of a parked car. Two women were patrolling the pavement. The air was warm and smelled relatively clean; for this night, at least, the rainy weather had washed exhaust fumes and male odours into the gutter.

Turkish music was playing behind a window. I took a

cigarette from my pack and noticed that I was out of matches.

'Need a light, darling?' One of the women planted herself in front of me and smiled. Thirtyish, she had a pretty but slightly fleshy face. Her white patent leather outfit didn't quite cover her ass, and her legs were encased in tall pointy boots.

I nodded, and she produced a lighter.

'Got an ashtray, too, upstairs.'

I shook my head. 'Thanks, but I'm waiting for somebody.'

She checked me out, from top to toe. 'You like the exotic types better? My roommate's the sweetest seductive thing since chocolate…'

I shook my head again. 'I told you, I'm just waiting for somebody.'

'For the guy you were with? Charlie's pet? You may have to wait a long time.'

'How so?'

'Cause he's a loser.'

I dragged on my cigarette, expelled the smoke through my nose, and shrugged. 'None of my business.'

'So why are you sitting here?'

'When he comes out, we'll go have a drink.'

'He's a buddy of yours?' She made a face. Then she looked me up and down again and asked, contemptuously: 'What kind of an asshole are you?'

Shaking her head, she strutted back to her beat. I watched her go, tossed my butt, got off the car trunk and went in. The joint was packed. Clouds of smoke hung under the ceiling, and the waiters' faces glistened with sweat. I made my way to the bar. Ignoring the instant angry chatter of the woman working the beer tap I opened the door marked Office and saw Schlumpi, the man I didn't know, and Slibulsky. Slibulsky's right cheek was red; now the left cheek turned the same colour.

'Kayankaya! Oh, shit! Fuck off!'

I slammed the door shut behind me. The man I did not know pursed his lips, looked indignant. Schlumpi wiggled his fingers and very carefully moved a little to one side. I opened my jacket to show the handles of the guns I was still wearing tucked behind my belt. 'Take a good look before you make a mistake.'

Schlumpi froze, and the man I didn't know cleared his throat.

'Such manners…' Suddenly I knew him, all right – I recognised his voice.

'Is it better manners to break someone's arm when he can't pay his debts?'

He was sitting behind a desk in a yellow and brown checked jacket, a pair of gold-rimmed spectacles on his nose, and some open ledgers in front of him. His hands were folded around a gold-plated ballpoint pen. He looked for all the world like a postal employee, maybe even a postmaster. One of those faceless types that make one wonder if they invented the rubber stamp or if the rubber stamp invented them.

'I don't know what you're talking about.'

'I'll explain it to you. Slibulsky here lost a bunch of money he inherited, fifty thousand marks to be exact, at your roulette table. And since he is a goddamn idiot, he then went on to borrow the next fifty thou, or whatever, from you, and proceeded to lose those as well. So now you're giving him the business, and he gets involved in a lot of bad shit in order to pay you back. You follow me?'

'Kayankaya…' Slibulsky sighed.

Ignoring him, I walked up to the guy to whom I had spoken on the phone the day before. I aimed my index finger at his nose. 'But here's the kicker. To whom does he owe that money, and for whom are you collecting? For Wang. And who are you? You are Eberhard Schmitz's secretary. We spoke yesterday. Now the fifty-thousand-mark question is: where has Wang been hiding since his wife was strangled and her lover fell out of the window? Even the cops should be able to find an answer to that. And while you're mulling that over, Schlumpi can tell the croupier…' I turned, '… to fix the wheel so that our numbers come up when we're playing.'

A pause. Schlumpi looked at the secretary, the secretary looked at me, I looked at Slibulsky, and Slibulsky looked at the ceiling. Then the secretary gave Schlumpi a nod, and Schlumpi left the office.

'I admit that you've got the edge, for now. But don't forget the consequences. How will Mr Wang react to this? He can change his residence quickly. I can foresee a few problems for you.'

Slibulsky almost managed to nod and shake his head at the same time. I did the latter.

'We won't have any problems. This is mainly a matter of principle. No one should think they can get away with just about anything merely because Wang isn't here. And that is why Slibulsky will recoup his losses in plain view of everybody. The alternative? Well, I'm a private investigator, and for twenty thousand marks I'll be glad to find Wang for you.'

He rolled the pen between his fingers, looking pensive. Then he shrugged and started closing the ledgers. 'As you wish. I'll inform Mr Wang about all of this. The rest will take care of itself.'

After he had stuffed the ledgers into a brown briefcase, he got up and walked around the desk. He moved jerkily, as if he had trouble retaining his posture without a backrest. 'As for you, Mr Slibulsky... Please accept my apologies for the business with your arm. It was done according to orders, and, as you must have noticed, I found it hard to observe.' Looking mildly embarrassed, he held out his hand to Slibulsky. 'No offence...'

Amazed, Slibulsky raised his eyebrows. Then he made an awkward gesture, and I had a hard time keeping a straight face. The secretary turned red in the face.

Armed with beer and shots of schnapps and a stack of blue chips we took our places at the roulette table. I leaned closer to Slibulsky: 'How much do we have to win here?'

'A hundred and twenty thousand.' And, while he was stacking the chips: 'How did you know about my inheritance?'

'Gina told me.'

'Mhm... And what would you have done if the guy hadn't happened to be Schmitz's secretary?'

'No idea.'

He divided the stack in two and shoved one half over to me. 'But I told you to keep out of it.'

'Go fuck yourself.'

I took the chips, leaned back, and bet a thousand on Odd.

The croupier, a lean guy with a moustache and cold eyes, glanced at both of us. Then he set the ball in motion and did not pay any attention to us for the next hour. It almost seemed as if he didn't even notice where we placed out bets. But he did notice, and when we left the joint around two o'clock, Slibulsky no longer owed the house a dime.

It was still warm outside. The moon had risen above the railway station. The woman in white patent leather was gone. We started walking to Raoul's Haiti-Corner, a small restaurant that served good rum and good beans. For a while we trundled along in silence. Slibulsky had stuck his left hand inside his coat and hunched his shoulders. As we left the railway quarter and turned into a side street, he finally spoke up: 'All right, you win. But the next time you think you have to pull me out of some shit, please let me know beforehand.'

I stopped.

'Just like you did, "let me know," eh?'

'How could I tell you anything? After you called me a guy who steals people's last pair of socks and then sends them off to be killed?'

'Touché. But just *tell* me next time – before you lose a fortune at roulette, and before you try to work for guys like Charlie in order to make some money for guys like Schlumpi, while Schmitz and Wang sit in their castle and wipe their asses with paper currency.'

He frowned. After a moment's silence, he said: 'Yes, you've got a point there.'

We walked on, faster. Our steps regained some of the old bounce. My stomach was growling as if I hadn't eaten anything for days.

As we passed Ellermann's Gaming and Sports centre with its third-floor pool hall, Slibulsky said: 'Maybe I should practise shooting with my left? I'm out of a job now anyway. We play as a team, and people like to bet against guys with casts on their arms. We let them win the first few games, then we up the ante, and all of a sudden —'

'Sure, sure. But you keep forgetting that you aren't so hot even with your right hand —'

'Not *there*, for crissakes! No, we'll do it in those joints where the yuppies like to spend an evening poking holes in the baize, with their girlfriends watching, and so on. Those guys tend to be pretty timid and tight-fisted, but when they see a hundred per cent chance to make a killing, they're worse than *Hausfraus* at a white sale! Gina once dragged me to a class reunion or whatever it was. Those guys don't just drink their beers: they *count* 'em. When the waiter comes to collect, each one of them knows down to the pfennig how much he and everyone else has had to drink. I'm sure they're terrific at skat. But if one of the party hasn't been keeping track, they pounce on him like hyenas. When I said I couldn't remember how many I'd had, so I'd be willing to make up the difference, three of them put in quick orders for food.'

We climbed over a railing beside the tram tracks and ran across.

'So how big would those bets be? Ten marks, and a fake term paper?'

'No. Those guys do have folding money in their secret little wallets. They pay for their drinks with small change, but just check out their threads – you could buy a house with what they cost. It's those little wallets we're after.'

'All right, we can give it a try. Practice at Ellermann's tomorrow night?'

Slibulsky scratched his neck. 'Don't know about tomorrow night... Maybe I'd better make myself scarce for a while – at least until we find out if Charlie will keep his mouth shut. And that Manne is a violent son of a bitch. When he finds out that his jig is up, he's liable to do anything. That wasn't a bad trick, by the way.'

'No, not bad.'

'Except that Manne doesn't wear a watch, but I only realised that later.'

'But why a gay joint?'

'Because I couldn't think of any other that far away. Charlie had told me about it. He said they filmed the patrons there, and then...' He rubbed his index finger with his thumb. 'I thought it would be a good false track, farfetched enough for you to stick with it for a while. And, besides –' he punched my shoulder playfully, 'one should try everything once.'

'Thanks but no thanks.'

'I read something about that in a paper. It said everybody's a little queer, so if you just do a little soul-searching, you'll discover that little bit in yourself. Jeez, people must have a lot of time – to search their souls to find out what it is they really need for a good time...'

'Just imagine what their good times consist of.'

We turned a corner and passed a tavern in which people were roaring the German national anthem. Two fat pimply-faced kids with shaved heads stood guard on either side of the door, holding wooden clubs at beer-belly level. The bomber jacket one of them was wearing bore a legend in black, red, and gold lettering; it said Keep Germany Beautiful – No Miscegenation!

Slibulsky said, in a loud voice: 'Know the one about the three Nazis getting a haircut?'

The kids' heads turned irritably. For a moment, they seemed to be contemplating action, but then they resumed their pose, staring dully straight ahead and pretending that they hadn't heard anything. Compulsion to obey orders.

'How does it go?'

'Yeah, right. The barber asks the first one how he'd like to have his hair cut, and the guy says "Parted on the right, like Hitler's." He asks the second one; he says "Shave it." Then he asks the third guy. He looks a little perplexed but says, quickly: "Like the others."'

We were the only patrons of the Haiti-Corner. Raoul joined us and treated us to a bottle of rum. After we had eaten and finished that bottle, we opened and worked on another one until Raoul locked the door and closed the blinds. Then we started rolling the dice. The loser had to propose a toast and down a shot of rum. Each game lasted five minutes.

Chapter 16

I sat at the kitchen table in my bathrobe, breakfasting on black coffee and pickled herring. The window was open. Radiant sunshine, blue sky. A warm wind caressed my face. In the street, a car radio blared 'Bella, bella, bella Marie'. That noise was interspersed by shouted orders: 'Gertrud! Turn the water on!' and 'Gertrud! Turn it off!' The first spring day of the year. My cabeza felt like it was made of lead.

I managed to swallow two rollmops and a cup of coffee. I got up, lit a cigarette, and leaned on the windowsill. People on their lunch break and housewives carrying bags streamed down the pavements, a gang of kids was sitting on a pile of building materials, spitting in front of their feet, and a miniskirt stood leaning against the bus stop sign. I watched the greengrocer pop out of his store to berate a woman about touching his wares. Then the phone rang. I pulled myself together, padded back into the room and flopped into my chair.

'Kayankaya.'

'Good morning. This is Elsa Sandmann. I woke up in your car, yesterday morning.'

'Oh…' I sat up straight. The party angel. Even though I hadn't forgotten her, I had hardly expected a call. Her voice was pleasantly hoarse, and I could tell she was puffing on a cigarette between phrases.

'I thought you might like to know how I ended up there.'

'Well, let's see… You had left that party; you were rather drunk, and you wanted me to take you to Frankfurt. But I had to go somewhere else – so you just got in and crashed in the back seat. When I came back, I tried to wake you up, but without success.'

'You weren't at that party?'

'No. I just happened to be there, on the street.'

'And then you just left me and drove off into the woods?'

'That's it, more or less. I did put a blanket over you.'

'Pretty strange, I must say.'

'Yes, it was. I had to leave you again. And then I was locked up. And then I got arrested.'

'Your card says you're a private investigator.'

'I know. After all, it was me who had those printed up.' After a brief pause that gave me the impression there was a smile at the other end of the line, she asked: 'But I always thought cops and private detectives were in cahoots?'

'You don't watch enough television.'

'That's possible. I also thought that detectives really needed their cars. But in your case, I suppose the suspects would have to help push.'

'Well, it's my kind of car.'

'Have you been looking for it?'

'No.'

'But I've been looking for you. After I had checked out the woods and every tavern in Gellersheim, I decided it would make more sense to drive to your place. I had no idea what that would involve. I stalled three times, the fourth gear wasn't working, and the brakes – well, all right. When I got to my place, I was exhausted. That car isn't just your kind of car, it doesn't even like strangers.'

'Oh, no. I'm sure it just got too excited by having you drive it. How about giving me your address, and I'll come and get it.'

Instead of giving me her address, she blew smoke into the mouthpiece. In the background I could hear street noises and the bell of a tram. I imagined that she was sitting there by a window, in her bathrobe, a plate of croissants in front of her.

I saw the sunlight glinting in her hair.

'When?'

'Tonight.'

She thought it over. A cup clinked against a saucer. 'Between seven and eight?'

'That's fine,' I said. She gave me an address in Sachsenhausen. Then we said ciao and hung up. It occurred to me that the telephone was as poor a setting for Elsa Sandmann as the rotting back seat of my car had been. Then again, none of us are too good on the phone, especially not when speaking to strangers: as often as not, the result is a chain of misunderstandings, inappropriate laughter, and pauses in which neither one knows whose turn it is to speak next.

I went back to the kitchen to study the street some more until the mailman arrived and handed me a large brown envelope. I ripped off the tape and pulled out a pink file folder, labelled in black magic marker: Rakdee, Sri Dao. Besides unimportant bits of paper including an Interpol printout that reported 'no data,' the file contained the following entries:

'Mrs Sri Dao Rakdee entered the Federal Republic of Germany on June twenty-second, nineteen hundred eighty-eight, on a tourist visa… applied on September twenty-second for an extension of visa in order to marry Mr Manfred Greiner.

'A further extension was granted on December twenty-second, nineteen hundred eighty-eight, after a delay encountered in efforts to obtain documents necessary for the marriage from Mrs Rakdee's birthplace, Chiang Mai.'

It was one of those old buildings freshly painted in candy colours that make one praise one's lucky stars for having plain old grey facades across the street. Day-Glo turquoise stripes on a yellow background with pink window frames. As if that weren't enough, every balcony was overflowing with potted palms and other plant life, helium balloons, children's toys turning in the wind, and all kinds of other tchotchkes. A blend of 'Dear Neighbour, Anarchy is Doable' and 'Our Village, Ever More Beautiful.'

I walked to the front door, which was off to one side

under a glass awning, and into the entrance hall. A gigantic chandelier hung from the ceiling. The staircase was carpeted in red. An advertising agency occupied the second floor, and on the third was a branch office of the Party That Has a Heart for Trees. That door was covered with stickers: North Sea, Nuclear power plants, Bicycles, Peace, Mandela, Palestinians, Nicaragua, Children, The Disabled, Gays, Gay Foreigners, Women, Pregnant Women, Single Women, Women in Houses of Prostitution… The door looked like a cross between a votive picture of the Virgin and a collection box for good causes, albeit one in which one needn't put anything. A prolonged glance was enough to receive absolution for all of last week's asocial actions and a moral advance against any that one might commit in weeks to come. To have these stickers on your door or car had to be the equivalent of a hundred Hail Marys.

I went on up to the fourth floor and rang the bell. There was no response. I rang again. When I heard someone approach on silent cat's feet, I moved out of spy hole range. After a while I rang a third time and heard a quiet, whiny voice say: 'Who is it?'

'Kayankaya. Let me in.'

'What do you want?'

'I want to talk to you.'

'We don't have anything to discuss.'

'I beg to differ. And if you don't let me in, I'll tell you everything from right here.' I raised my voice. 'It's just that I'd be sharing it with the whole building, and I don't know –'

The door opened and Weidenbusch stood there in pale

blue pyjamas made out of some kind of towelling fabric. He was blushing. 'I must say, this is —'

I touched my forehead. 'Good morning.'

Then I pushed past him into the apartment, crossed a shiny parquet floor, and stopped in a large, sunny room. Weidenbusch followed, yapping at my heels: 'You're trespassing! As a detective, you ought to know that!'

Then he stopped in the doorway and fussed with his hair. The room was decorated with the kind of art that looks as if someone had decided, one morning, to paint his breakfast tray white and hang it on the wall. In the middle stood a table with weird angles, surrounded by chairs shaped like stylised lightning bolts. And there were dozens of lamps. Each one of them resembled something that didn't look the least bit like a light fixture. Otherwise the room seemed empty, until I took a quick tour of it and discovered a television set, discreetly hidden behind the door. The windows were open, and strains of Asiatic folk tunes could be heard from outside.

I turned: 'Is it possible to sit on one of those?'

He didn't get that right away. Then he responded, sounding a little annoyed: 'But of course. They're as stable as any common chair. My cousin designed those.' He added, looking blasé: 'Unfortunately, you can now see them in every other apartment.' But I could tell that he was putting a brave face aboard a ship the rats were abandoning in a hurry.

'Gosh, I must only visit the ones that don't have them yet.'

I sat down on one of the lightning bolts, took out my cigarettes and matches and put them on the table.

'I haven't asked you to stay.'

'Thanks, but I don't need an invitation. Boy, you must be a real tight family. The furniture's designed by a cousin, your mother makes decisions about your girlfriend…' I looked at him. 'But that, of course, was a lie.'

He hurried over to the table. 'I told you at the airport – you're no longer working for me! And if you're trying to get more money out of me…' He picked up my smoking paraphernalia and tossed them in my lap. 'The cheque's in the mail. And that's all you'll get from me.'

'Listen, brillo pad, how come you're acting so superior all of a sudden? Have you been taking lessons? But you're missing something here.'

I put cigarettes and matches back on the table.

'You still haven't told me if you found Mrs Rakdee yesterday.'

He opened his mouth, but I raised my hand and shook my head. His face was turning paler.

'Pretty clever, I must say. The artsy little fellow who gets cold feet on a foray into real life and then lets Mum whip him back into his customary existence in one of these nice old buildings. I really bought it. With the greatest of ease.'

He was still standing in front of me in the get-out-of-here mode, but now he was staring at the floor, and his terry-cloth-covered belly was heaving rapidly.

'How about offering me a cup of coffee?'

He looked up. 'Coffee?' He looked absent-minded, then shook his head. 'My espresso machine is broken.'

'I'm not that choosy. Just make some with a filter.'

'I have no filters.'

'You don't? All right, tea or cocoa will do. And get your girlfriend. I'm sure she'd like to have some breakfast, and I'll only be a minute.'

He stared at me. His face lost all colour, and for a moment it looked as if he would attack me. His voice was trembling. 'You're hallucinating. Get out of my house!' Then he panicked, and he raised his arms. 'I don't want to see you any more! Ever again! Just go! Get out of here!'

I got up and slapped him. He yelped and covered his face with his hands.

'Stop the hysterics. I'm here to wind up a case. And if you'd stop to think for a second, you would notice that I haven't brought any cops or handcuffs. You and your girlfriend will be perfectly safe.'

He lowered his arms. Tears were running down his cheeks.

'Wh-what?'

'You heard me.' I sat down again and pointed at the second door in the room. 'She's listening to us, right behind that door, isn't she? So, pull yourself together, for her sake if nothing else.'

He needed a couple more minutes during which nothing was heard except for his heavy breathing and the jangling of folk tunes. Then he gulped, turned, and called out in English:

'Sweetheart, please come in!'

The door opened slowly, and a woman in her mid-twenties, in a red and white striped cotton dress, entered the room. She was barely five foot tall, delicately built, and had a round, apple-cheeked face with large serious eyes, framed by shoulder-length black hair. Her feet, encased in yellow raffia slippers, made no sound as she came forward, arms folded across her chest. 'Good morning.'

'Good morning.' I nodded, then asked Weidenbusch: 'Now will you get us something to drink?'

Ten minutes later, Weidenbusch was pouring tea into our cups. After that initial greeting Sri Dao had not uttered a single word. She observed events with complete calm and followed our conversation with interest. There was no way of telling how much she understood or what she thought of it. After Weidenbusch had taken a seat at the table, I began my story: the visa scam, and Charlie, and Höttges, and Manne Greiner. At first, I addressed Sri Dao directly, but when that seemed more and more like talking to a wall, I concentrated on Weidenbusch.

'... so my first impression was correct: when the VW bus arrived, Mrs Rakdee recognised her former husband and pimp. But it was not an intentional reunion. It was a mistake. I assume that Charlie made the necessary calls and sent Manne to the agreed pick-up point without giving him any names. So the surprise was mutual, and if the gang didn't want to endanger the anonymity of their operation, they had to get rid of Mrs Rakdee. I don't know what plans they had for her, but when the group was moved out of the villa, Manne stayed behind –with her.'

I sipped my tea. If Weidenbusch hadn't been heaving the occasional mournful sigh, one would have thought that he had fainted while sitting there with wide open eyes. Sri Dao, on the other hand, was desultorily stirring the sugar in the sugar bowl.

'Then, when I got there, only Manne was left. Dead –

and in a state of undress customarily assumed only by couples. He may have raped Mrs Rakdee, or she may have seduced him. Whatever was the case, she had managed to break his neck.'

Weidenbusch gave me a quick glance. Then he leaned forward and rested his forehead on his hands. Sri Dao watched his movements and looked surprised.

'After that, she called you. But she didn't tell you about the murder. Then you called me at home, but I wasn't there. When we had our next telephone conversation, you already knew what had happened. You wanted me to stop my investigation, and, as I told you, I almost believed your change of heart. But when you showed up at the airport to demonstrate once again, and in person, how ignorant you were of Mrs Rakdee's whereabouts, it became obvious to me that a) someone was pressuring you – but there was nothing to go on in that direction, or b) you had your own reasons for leading me down a false trail. And so on, and so forth. All in all, it's not a bad theory, and that's all it is. There is no evidence, and I won't go looking for any. There isn't even a corpse. I buried it, because I assumed from the start that the murder could only have been committed by a refugee who gained his – or her – freedom. In my book that's self-defence, even if other motives may have come into play.' I paused briefly, then said: 'Now do you understand what I meant by saying nothing will happen to you?'

But he didn't understand, at least not immediately. He was still hiding his face in his hands. Next to him, Sri Dao contemplated her own hands which lay folded in her lap. I picked up my teacup and leaned back. The first bees of spring hummed into the room, and you could hear children laughing and bouncing balls down in the street. Maybe Elsa Sandmann would accept an invitation to have dinner with me?

Slowly, Weidenbusch raised his head. 'But why did you come here, to tell us these things, if you –'

'If I don't intend to do anything about it? First of all, it was my job to find Mrs Rakdee. That's what you were paying me for. Now I have found her. Second, I've been involved in this story for too long not to feel the urge to tell it at least once. And third, I don't enjoy being fooled. So,' I took out my wallet and put three thousand-mark bills on the table, 'here's your money.'

'Oh!' He waved it aside. 'No, no, you keep it, please. I don't know how else to thank you… If that's the right expression – what I mean is…'

There was still fear in his voice, and I began to wonder what he might need to regain his balance. Maybe his girlfriend ought to give him a hug, I thought. But, for a while now, she had been casting a rather cool eye at him, just as if he had committed some kind of blunder. As far as I could see, he hadn't been doing anything besides stammering incoherently. Being a murderess safe from prison, and seeming quite unconcerned about her deed, I felt that she could have been a little nicer to him. I took one of the bills, said 'That's fine,' and prepared to leave. As I picked up my cigarettes I happened to glance at the daily paper lying next to them. In the lower right-hand corner was the result of the tennis game Becker vs. Steeb, two days ago. Six two, six two for Becker. Suddenly I understood Sri Dao's unfriendly mood. If Slibulsky hadn't seen the end of the game but had answered Weidenbusch's phone call, not more than half an hour could have elapsed between my departure and that call. This would have been just enough time for Slibulsky to raise the alarm in Gellersheim and to have the villa evacuated in a panic mode. But it was not enough time for a murder and two phone calls. In other words: by whatever means Sri Dao had managed to reach a phone in that chaos, she must have called Weidenbusch during the evacuation. And when Weidenbusch hadn't been able to reach me, he himself had driven to Gellersheim.

I looked at the couple. Both of them seemed tense. Weidenbusch interpreted my hesitation in his customary manner and said quickly: 'No, just take it all, and if you would like more –'

'Stay where you are.'

Her elbow on the table, Sri Dao was holding her cup under her nose and watching him and me across the rim as if we were playing ping-pong.

'I think that Mrs Rakdee feels you should tell me something.'

He looked irritated, turned to look at her. 'Sweetheart?'

Sweetheart did not react.

'What do you mean by that?'

'Well, maybe it isn't such a good start for a wonderful love affair if one party lets the other get away with murder.'

He opened his mouth. Then he nodded, slowly.

Ten minutes later, Weidenbusch had smoked three cigarettes while telling me how he had arrived at the villa, how he had snuck down into the basement, and how he had seen Manne Greiner raping Sri Dao. What followed was pure reflex – a knee between the prone man's shoulders, a firm grip on his forehead, and a powerful tug to snap his neck.

His voice grew firmer as he spoke. He stubbed his cigarette in the ashtray and for the first time in our acquaintance seemed almost calm. 'I wouldn't have thought you could do that.'

He shrugged. 'Me neither. So. Are you going to hand me over to the cops?'

'No.' I pocketed my cigarettes. 'Just don't start writing a poem about it when you're back in shape.'

I was about to get up when Sri Dao grabbed my arm and pointed at the newspaper with a questioning expression. I tapped the tennis results with my finger. She looked perplexed. Then the doorbell rang. Weidenbusch stared at me. I ran to the window. A green and white van stood in the carriageway.

'Police. I'll take care of them. But you better think of something to get her visa extended. Good luck.'

'But,' Weidenbusch cleared his throat, 'I mean, won't I see you again?'

Without turning, and casting a final glance at the painted breakfast trays, I replied: 'That's entirely up to you. As you know, it's two hundred a day plus expenses.'

I opened the door. There were four of them: three in uniform and one in plain clothes. The plainclothes guy had a friendly face adorned by a moustache. We looked at each other with a degree of amazement.

'Goodness, Inspector, what are you doing here?'

'That's what I wanted to ask you.'

I pulled the door shut behind me. 'This is my new apartment.'

Klaase craned his neck to read the nameplate. 'Oh – but what about Mr Weidenbusch?'

'I think he moved to Munich. Why?'

'Well, because…' He unfolded a sheet of paper. The uniformed guys were looking at me in a manner indicating that as far as they were concerned, it was a criminal offence for me to be walking on two legs.

'I have here a deportation order against a Mrs Sri Dao Rakdee. And we've been informed that she resides here.'

I shrugged. 'I don't know her. You coming down with me?'

Descending the stairs we exchanged the usual How-Are-You-Thanks-All-Right-Weekend-Coming-Up-Thank-God platitudes. But once we were on the pavement, Klaase took me aside, waving the uniformed guys back into the van.

'I hope you treated the information I gave you confidentially?'

'But of course.'

He didn't look totally convinced. 'This morning Höttges asked me if I had told anybody about Gellersheim.'

'Really? Speaking of Höttges – you said such a kind thing about him when we talked on the phone: something to the effect that he'd had a hard life. What were you referring to?'

'Oh, that…' He cleared his throat, seemed reluctant. 'I don't have any details, exactly.'

'How about some inexact details?'

'Well… he was always so proud of his family, a happy marriage, three kids… but then it all turned bad. Because of infidelities.'

'He doesn't look like a womaniser.'

'That's just it.'

'… I see.'

We walked to the van. The uniformed guys watched us through the windows, talking to each other.

'You should change that name plate.'

'Yes, the super's been at me about that for two days.' I patted his shoulder. 'So, keep up the good work. Keep an eye out for things.'

He smiled hesitantly. 'Thanks.'

I grinned. 'Don't mention it. Goodbye.'

'Bye.'

I turned and walked down the street. It was still a warm day with blue skies. I took off my jacket and slung it over my shoulder. My wallet now contained a cheque for twenty thousand marks and Weidenbusch's thousand. My first purchase was an ice cream cone, and while the vendor scoured the neighbourhood to get me my change, I stopped in the chemist next door and picked out a pair of sunglasses, whistling 'Say a Little Prayer for You.' It was easy to whistle with that kind of money in my pocket. I wouldn't be doing it for very long.

I unlocked the door to my office, tossed the mail and newspapers into the clients' chair, and opened the windows, letting in a blend of odour: vanilla and frying fat. The Chicken Inn across the street had put its soft-ice machine out on the pavement. I went to the sink, rinsed a glass, took the bottle of Chivas out of the desk drawer and helped myself to a generous drink. Then I stood by the window, sipping Scotch and letting the sun shine on my face. I had finished the job, and the next couple of weeks, I thought, I could do as I pleased. Sleep, play billiards, sit in cafes, perhaps even take a drive out into the countryside. Eat some good food, smoke good cigarettes at eight marks a pack. And I would ask Gina if she knew the name of that book about the old guy in the sewers of Paris. Maybe, at long last, I'd even hop on a plane headed south. For a week or two, if not longer.

I finished my drink and was about to check the mail when the phone rang.

'Mr Kayankaya?'

'Yes?'

'Olschewski here. Mr Schmitz would like to talk to you.' The line crackled. I hurried to refill my glass and pulled a cigarette from the pack. Then Schmitz's distinguished voice came on the line. 'Good afternoon, Mr Kayankaya. I've been reading the papers, and I gather that several dozen refugees were found in a bunker in Gellersheim, where they had been taken from some otherwise unspecified villa. I assume that you were the source of that information?'

'Let's just say that I made sure the newspapers were able to talk to those refugees.'

'So you forgot what I explained to you?'

'You mean that thing about the difference…' I lit my cigarette, took a deep drag, blew the smoke out. 'It really isn't that great. You're doing your job as best you can, and I'm doing mine to the best of my ability. Beyond that, it's just a question of how many gilded objects one wants in one's house, and whether one really needs a flunkey at the door. I have no objections to that, but I like to open and close my own doors. If you think you need to get rid of me, you'll have to hire killers to do it. But if I blow the whistle on you, I'll do it in person – either because I want to, or because I'm forced to do it. So, let's see who gets more ambitious.'

'You're threatening me?'

'I'm just letting you know what I think of your little lecture the other night. I'm doing my job, and if you attack me because of that, I'll defend myself. I may just kick you in the shins, but, who knows, I might even land one on your head.'

He cleared his throat, then asked, with a pretence of mild amusement: 'Seems almost as if you'd been waiting for me to call.'

'I've been counting on it.'

'Well, I really should be mad at you, but I think you're quite a guy. After our conversation I didn't think you'd pursue that affair. To tell the truth, I didn't get my information only from the newspapers. Mr Köberle told me everything.'

I felt a lump in my throat. 'Everything?'

'How you took the money back from the gang. Very brave, one against three. Which brings us to the main reason for my call. I would like to hire you.'

Was the whisky that strong this afternoon, or was I dreaming?

'Excuse me?'

'You heard me. It concerns my nephew Axel. You met

him. I admit that he's a disaster in every respect, but for the last twenty years, he has always showed up on time for our little talks. Until this morning. Mr Köberle tells me that after your show at the garage last night, he drove Axel home. But he isn't there. I've spent the morning making calls, but I haven't been able to reach him. Frankly, I'm worried about what may have happened to him. There are these Yugoslavs who are trying to muscle in on my business – I'll tell you the details when you come over. In any case, I want you to find my nephew. And I suppose that the cheque I gave you – which did not fulfill its original purpose – would do as a retainer.'

While listening to him I had helped myself to a big gulp of Scotch and made myself comfortable behind the desk.

'Sorry, but I can't take that on.'

'Why not?'

'I'm in training for a billiards tournament.'

'You're joking.'

'No, I'm not.'

I looked out the window. A vapour trail stretched across the sky, heading south. Then Schmitz asked, pretending to be casual about it: 'Have you cashed that cheque?'

I knew what he had in mind, and I knew that I could keep the twenty thousand if I said 'Yes.' I didn't really know why I said 'No.'

'Well… Come to think of it, there's no dead body in Gellersheim, and there's no way you could take that refugee story to the cops… '

He paused, just in case he was wrong and I would tell him so. But he wasn't wrong, and he went on to say: 'So I guess I'll stop payment on it.'

'Do that. You'll have more money that way.'

He laughed. 'Right you are. Goodbye.' He hung up. I stared into space for a while. Then I took half of Weidenbusch's money, stuck it into an envelope with a note that said 'Kayankaya's rent' and wrote Kunze's address on the envelope. After which I started cleaning up the office. I vacuumed and swept, washed dishes, took the garbage downstairs.

With a replenished glass of Scotch I sat down at my clean desk and opened my mail. A subpoena to be a witness at a trial – the case was two months old; an advertising circular from a weapons firm; a 'League for a Future Palestine' wanted to know if they could hire me as a bodyguard… I began to read sentences three or four times without comprehension. Finally I put the rest of the unopened mail aside and leaned back in my chair. This was no day for routine, no matter how hard I'd try. Tomorrow would be such a day, and so would the day after tomorrow, and the days to come, but today even the sight of my name on those envelopes was too much. I took Schmitz's cheque out of my wallet and leaned it against the base of my desk lamp. It looked good there. Then I finished my drink and got up.

A little after two o'clock I left the brown office building and headed downtown. At the first refreshment stand I purchased some cigarettes for eight marks a pack. In six hours I would have my date with Elsa Sandmann, and it looked like the weather would stay warm and nice until then. I would find a quiet cafe with an outdoor terrace, maybe even one with a small billiard table in the back. I could practise a few massé shots. The tournament was in three weeks, and since Slibulsky was only half a player now, I had to get twice as good.

I paid, put on my new shades, and walked down the street. The high-rise buildings gleamed above the American barracks, and the air smelled of tar and burnt rubber.

OTHER KEMAL KAYANKAYA TITLES

also available as ebooks

Happy Birthday, Turk!
£9.99
The First Kemal Kayankaya Mystery

A Turkish worker – Ahmed Hamul – is stabbed to death in
Frankfurt's red-light district – certainly no reason for the local
police to work overtime. But when the labourer's wife comes to
him for help, PI Kemal Kayankaya, a Turkish immigrant himself
with first hand experience of resentment against foreigners, smells
a rat.

More Beer
£9.99
The Second Kemal Kayankaya Mystery
Four members of a radical ecological group are accused of the
murder of the director of a chemical plant near Frankfurt. While
admitting to material damage of the plant they deny any
involvement with the murder. According to witnesses, five people
participated in the sabotage but where is the fifth man? The
defendant's lawyer hires Kemal Kayankaya to find him.

Born in Turkey but raised in Germany, Kayankaya encounters
many obstacles in his search to unravel the complex riddle at the
heart of this mystery, not only because he is a Turk but also
because his acidic wit spares no one, not even the political and
judicial powers who seem will stop at nothing to try and silence
him...

Kismet
£9.99
The Fourth Kemal Kayankaya Mystery

It all began with a favour. Kayankaya and Slibulsky were only trying to protect their friend Romario from men demanding hard cash. It ended with two bodies on the floor of Romario's restaurant, their faces covered in ghostly white make-up.

Kayankaya is determined to track down their identity, but realises that is being pursued by a faceless but utterly ruthless criminal gang. A new element has broken into the established order of Frankfurt gangland: Croatian nationalists, battle hardened from the wars in their homeland. And when Kayankaya rescues a teenage Bosnian girl, Leila, from what purports to be a refugee hostel. . . the stakes get even higher.

Brother Kemal
£7.99
The Fifth Kemal Kayankaya Mystery

Valerie de Chavannes, a financier's daughter, asks private investigator Kemal Kayankaya to find her missing sixteen-year-old, Marieke. She is alleged to be with an older man who is posing as an artist. To Kayankaya, it seems like a simple case: an upper class girl with a thirst for adventure.

Then another case turns up: The Maier Publishing House believes it needs to protect author Malik Rashid from attacks by religious fanatics at the Frankfurt Book Fair. The two cases seem to be straightforward, but together they lead to murder, rape and abduction, and even Kayankaya comes under suspicion of being a contract killer for hire.

About Us

In addition to No Exit Press, Oldcastle Books has a number of other imprints, including Pulp! The Classics, Kamera Books, Creative Essentials, Pocket Essentials and High Stakes Publishing.

For more information, media enquiries and review copies please contact Alexandra Bolton, alexandra@oldcastlebooks.com

FIND OUT MORE ABOUT OLDCASTLE BOOKS

www.oldcastlebooks.co.uk